The Beothuk Expedition

DEREK YETMAN

The Beothuk EXPEDITION

Copyright © 2011 Derek Yetman

All Rights Reserved. No part of this publication may be reproduced, stored in a retrieval system or transmitted, in any form or by any means, without the prior written consent of the publisher or a licence from The Canadian Copyright Licensing Agency (Access Copyright). For an Access Copyright licence, visit www.accesscopyright.ca or call toll freeto 1-800-893-5777.

Yetman, Derek, 1955-
The Beothuk expedition / Derek Yetman.
ISBN 978-1-55081-360-9
1. Cartwright, George, 1739-1819 – Fiction.
2. Beothuk Indians – Fiction. I. Title.
PS8597.E78B46 2011   C813'.54   C2011-906012-4

WWW.BREAKWATERBOOKS.COM
Breakwater Books is committed to choosing papers and materials for our books that help to protect our environment. To this end, this book is printed on a recycled paper that is certified by the Forest Stewardship Council of Canada.

 Canada Council for the Arts / Conseil des Arts du Canada   Canadä   Newfoundland Labrador

We acknowledge the support of the Canada Council for the Arts which last year invested $20.1 million in writing and publishing throughout Canada. We acknowledge the Government of Canada through the Canada Book Fund and the Government of Newfoundland and Labrador through the Department of Tourism, Culture and Recreation for our publishing activities.

PRINTED AND BOUND IN CANADA.

Printed on Silva Enviro 100% post-consumer EcoLogo certified paper, processed chlorine free and manufactured using biogas energy.

for Brenda

On the 15th day of August, in

Lieutenant Jonah Squibb of H

embark upon a voyage that would fore

had been at sea from a tender age and k

less of the cruelty that men

their fellow beings. I had fought

suffering, but at least our enemies had

science of war. Nothing I had known

me for the inhumanity to which I bore

It was a cruelty that had no greater

than to destroy a helpless race of peopl

On the 15th day of August, in the year of Our Lord 1768, I, Lieutenant Jonah Squibb of His Majesty's Ship Guernsey, did embark upon a voyage that would forever change my view of humankind. I had been at sea from a tender age and knew little of the world at large, much less of the cruelty that men are willing to inflict upon their fellow beings. I had fought the French and seen my share of suffering, but at least our enemies had been equally armed and skilled in the science of war. Nothing I had known in my years at sea could have prepared me for the inhumanity to which I bore witness in that terrible summer of 1768. It was a cruelty that had no greater motive than profit, and no better purpose than to destroy a helpless race of people.

Jonah Squibb

The first faint aura of dawn seeped through the open ports, purple light giving shape and substance to the silent men around me. They were as I had imagined them in darkness, kneeling or crouching by the great guns, eyes straining for the first glimpse of their target in the foggy gloom. The cry of a gull and the creak of our timbers were the only sounds to disturb the awakening world. By slow degrees the shoreline emerged and the gun captains shifted their aim with a muffled clank of iron bars and the low rumble of wooden wheels.

Silence again as the shore grew distinct. I judged the moment with care and allowed another minute to pass. Then, at my nod, the gunner bellowed his command. His last word was neatly amputated by the deafening thunder of our quarter broadside. Teeth and eyeballs rattled in our skulls as the six great guns belched tongues of flame and shrieking metal. Behind it the din of shouting sailors and panicked livestock filled the air. Above it all, I heard the gunner cry: "Crows up, four!" Men and boys jumped to their tools, bare backs straining as number four gun, its barrel akimbo, was levered and cursed back onto its carriage.

"Swab and load!" roared the gunner. Smoke from the barrage drifted inboard, searing eyes and throats and obscuring my view of our target. A gap in the haze revealed it for an instant—

long enough for me to damn the sight of it: Every one of our eighteen-pound balls had gone wide or high, smashing into the wall of rock and causing a small avalanche of shale. I turned my attention inboard in time to see a terrified pig collide with the legs of a man carrying shot. Down he went, iron balls rumbling away and the squealing pig running harum scarum along the gundeck. A ship's boy abandoned his post and gave chase, narrowly dodging a vicious swipe from the marine guard. Boy and pig disappeared into the smoke and clamour as the guns, reloaded and primed, were run out for a second salvo. At my signal they bucked like iron horses, men clinging to the side tackles to check their recoil. The concussion entered my ears like a sailmaker's needle and through the billowing smoke I saw another half-dozen showers of rock fall from the face of the cliff.

A murmuring hush crept over the fifty-odd men as I gazed at the unmolested barrels that had been the object of our gunnery. I was not completely deaf, for I could still hear the pig, along with the hoots and jeers from the weather deck above us. I turned and not a man would meet my eye. The stench of powder, sweat and animal shit filled the airless space.

"House your guns, Mister Bolger," I sighed, loud enough for all to hear. "No doubt the enemy has injured himself with laughter." Sheepish grins and averted eyes were the only reply. "Powder to the magazine and see to number four straight away."

"Aye, aye, sir." The gunner touched his forehead with a dirty finger.

"And have the pigs and goats returned to the manger," I added.

The men cleared a path to the ladders and a moment later I emerged onto the upper deck and into daylight. I turned from the reproachful sight of the empty barrels on Southside Beach, reflecting that six years of peace had brought a new breed of sailor into the Navy—one who was slow to learn on what his survival depended. A pair of midshipmen walked past me, stifling grins as they made their way astern. On the quarterdeck, Mr. Tench, the second lieutenant, was gazing at the beach

The Beothuk Expedition

in smug amusement. I filled my pipe and moved to the larboard rail.

St. John's had changed but little since my last visit. A familiar eye could see that old Fort William had been strengthened and a new battery laid at Crow's Nest, though it was still the acres of drying fish that marked this outpost of empire. Wooden flakes ringed the harbour and blanketed the hills, their expanse broken here and there by a chimney or a roof. Such was the demand for space to dry fish that even the houses and roads were canopied with rough platforms, all laden with the salted wealth of the sea.

The harbour was now fully awake thanks to our antics, with schooners and brigs raising sail or signal or pumping their bilges. There was activity at every turn, for the ships were anchored only as long as it took to unload their catch or to stow the cured fish for a voyage to Portugal or the Indies. Gigs and dories moved among them, ferrying the men and supplies on which the fleet depended. My gaze moved along the hills and beyond the patchwork of flakes, to where tall stands of pine and spruce marked the edge of the island's great wilderness.

That dark and unexplored forest was the subject of much speculation amongst the men of my ship. Few of them had seen anything wilder than the park of an English manor, and tall tales and superstitions abounded on the lower decks, much to the amusement of the older hands. The Newfoundland woods were vast and unknown, to be sure, but as a boy I'd wandered freely there and seen nothing of the fairies or fearsome creatures conjured by simple minds. I smiled at the thought, unaware that the forest held things more terrible than even a sailor could imagine.

I was born on the Newfoundland station and, at the age of twenty-four, had spent much of my life at sea. I'd recently been posted as third lieutenant of the *Guernsey*, a fifty-gun man-of-war that had been launched well before my birth. Indeed, many judged her to be the slowest, leakiest tub in the whole of His Majesty's Navy, a distinction for which she had much competition. I'd sailed on her before, plying the Channel in pursuit of smugglers and keeping an eye on the French. It was in that storm-battered service that she'd become increasingly derelict. A cruise to the West Indies and a warm engagement with a Spanish privateer had done her no favours. Lately her poor joints had worked themselves loose and the movement of her parts required the rigging to be bowsed taut every other day. It was in this condition that she had sailed to the island as the flagship of Captain Hugh Palliser, the naval governor.

Our orders were to patrol the coast and to regulate the fishery, though in truth, the *Guernsey* spent as much time in port as she did at sea. Those long summer days of awaiting or undergoing repairs passed slowly for me, the ship being well manned and my duties light when we were not under sail. The officers stood their watches and went about a routine that was established by custom and decree, and yet I found time heavy upon my hands.

My principal distraction from the boredom of harbour life, aside from gunnery practice, was reading. I'd brought with me a number of books and with so few duties, had finished all but two of them. That very morning I'd resolved to read the remaining volumes in alternate fashion, in the vague hope of prolonging the pleasure. One was a fine octavo edition of Henry Fielding's *Journal of a Voyage to Lisbon*, full bound in polished calf. The other was a marbled board reprint of *Travels Through France and Italy*, from the former naval surgeon, Tobias Smollett. It was on the 15th day of August, the very day that we departed St. John's, that I began to read these narratives of travel in foreign parts. I had hoped to find in them a spiritual escape from the confines of the ship, but I was not to be so well rewarded. In fact, the authors' remarks on the human condition might well have been made from an observation of life on board the ancient *Guernsey*.

And so, on that August morning, as the sun rose and the shadows shortened, the order came to strike our moorings and prepare to sail on the falling tide. Boats were lowered and oarsmen bent to the task of towing our ship from the crowded harbour. I took my place on the quarterdeck, enjoying the first stir of excitement that precedes a welcome voyage. We passed through the anchorage in an orderly manner until we were into the Narrows and the boats were hoisted aboard. As the topsails fell, the deck came to life beneath our feet. Drawing abreast of the Devil's Cleft, that great vertical slash in the rock of Signal Hill, my ears fetched the roar of the sea from deep within. We were courting a westerly breeze, though faint, and once outside the Narrows, Mr. John Cartwright, our first lieutenant, called for all canvas. This was done handily enough, but my practiced eye detected a sloppy effort on the mainsail yard. One of the hands was a trifle slow in letting go his reefing lines and Frost, the boatswain, was quick to address him.

"Ahoy there, Greening!" he boomed. "Shall I send up your hammock, sir? Look lively, you whore's egg, or you'll know the taste of my rope, by God!" His words had their intended effect and young Greening scurried up the shroud to assist in setting the topgallant. I knew the lad to be Newfoundland born, and though he'd been raised on the water, he was unaccustomed to the precise workings of a man-o-war. But he did show promise, which was why the boatswain threatened him so frequently.

The *Guernsey* responded to the light airs as well as she could, her every timber groaning as the helm went over. For a long minute she wallowed indecisively. Then, ever so slowly, she turned her bow northward like an old whale that instinctively follows its path of migration. In fact, the ship had made the voyage north many times before and may have retained some sense of where her destination lay.

We settled on our course and I looked to the weather rail where Captain Palliser stood, his eyes hard fast upon the sails. He was a tall man of about forty-five years, his hair graying but his eyes as sharp as a seahawk's. I had come to know him as a fine seaman and a fair and reasonable officer in the bargain. He had been at sea from the age of eleven and had acquitted himself well as lieutenant of the *Essex* in an engagement off Toulon in 1744. He later took command of the *Weazle* sloop, where he found the sea room to demonstrate his full abilities. In short order he'd captured four French privateers, a feat that had earned him a captain's epaulets and command of a seventy-gun ship of war, all at the ripe old age of twenty-five. A misfortune befell him, however, on a cruise to Dominica. The ship's armourer carelessly struck fire to an arms chest, igniting the cartridge boxes and discharging every musket and pistol in the chest. The armourer and his mate were killed outright and the captain was badly wounded by three musket balls to the back, hip and shoulder. Having youth and health on his side, he recovered but remained lame in the left leg, and suffered great pain when the weather turned cold and damp.

In his five years as governor, Captain Palliser had introduced many improvements to the trade and defence of the colony, including new laws to govern shipping and a customs house for St. John's. And yet there were those who did not agree with his ideas or his methods of implementing them. These included the island's merchants, who were long accustomed to doing as they pleased. I was not familiar with all of his reforms but there was one that I would soon know more about.

Our destination that day was the harbour of Bonavista and I judged that it would take us a fortnight to get there in such an inferior breeze. Still, I was happy at the prospect of time to read my books and to study Mr. Cook's new coastal charts. That able gentleman had been the sailing master on my old ship, the *Northumberland*, in 1762, when he'd been kind enough to provide me with instruction in the navigational sciences. For that and for his patience, I was forever in his debt. Since that time James Cook had served the governor as marine surveyor of the island and Labrador. As master and commander of HMS *Grenville* he'd thoroughly charted the local waters, named harbours and even discovered new islands. The previous governor had persuaded the Admiralty to publish his charts, and now he was about to sail from Plymouth as captain of the *Endeavour*, bound for a lengthy cruise of exploration in the South Pacific. I was pleased that the reputation of my old teacher was so rapidly advancing.

The purpose of our own voyage that morning was to rendezvous with the frigate *Liverpool*, which was patrolling the northeast coast of the island. From Bonavista, we would proceed in company to the Isle of Fogo and join the other ships of the governor's squadron. These were the frigates *Lark* and *Tweed*, of thirty-two guns apiece, which were returning from provisioning the garrisons at Fort Pitt and Fort York in Labrador. Those new defences were another of Captain Palliser's ideas, undertaken to protect British interests and to prevent the French from trading with the natives. Another motive, no doubt, was to discourage settlement on that coast, for the governor viewed any increase in the year-round population as a threat to the Navy's supply of able seamen. Mr. Palliser was of the view that the migratory fishery was an ideal training ground for sailors, and those returning to England from the island were perfect candidates for recruiters or the press gangs. To me this seemed a flawed argument, for could not a larger resident population produce its share of sailors as well? And what of the benefits of year-round settlement to the colony's defence? Such lofty matters were not my concern, however, and my mind turned to other things as we altered course to greet a subtle change of wind.

I was happy to be at sea again and not only to escape the monotony of the harbour. In truth, I had a particular desire to leave St. John's because of melancholy thoughts that had troubled me while we lay at anchor. I had tried to ignore them but they were a constant shadow, plaguing me by day and disturbing my sleep at night. The reason for this was the memory of an event that had occurred there some six years before, on my last visit to the place. It was then that a letter had come into my hand, a letter that had served to change the course of my young life. It came from Amy Taverner, my childhood sweetheart at Trinity, and I had welcomed it with a joyful heart. My happiness was brief, however. I was not prepared for what she had written, not for the blow of learning that she had become engaged to another. My youthful world had collapsed like a mast shot through.

Derek Yetman

Because of that letter I had turned my back to Amy Taverner and to my home, giving my life over to the sea and to His Majesty's service. It was a life that suited me well enough, but after six years I had begun to pine for Newfoundland again. For what reason, I was at a loss to say. Was it the beauty of unspoiled Creation, the vast forests or the soaring capes and headlands? Or was it the very sea and air, those servants of nature's whims? It may have been the remembrance of my childhood or a longing for the happiness that I had been denied. In any event, I was drawn to this place as if by a spell, and more than once I'd felt like a fool for my attachment to this remote rock in the ocean. And yet the bond was real and the urge to return could not be ignored. But now I found it nearly as painful to be here as it had been to stay away. Six years had passed and still the wound refused to heal.

On this particular evening, I did as I'd done many times and tried to put thoughts of Amy Taverner from my mind. She was but a ghost from my past and one best forgotten if I was ever to be at peace again. Here now was the reality of my life—the lift of the *Guernsey*'s quarterdeck, the island to windward and the great expanse of sea rolling out to meet the sky. It was all that I could wish for, and yet my desire to believe it did not make my heart grow lighter.

St. John's fell away as we lumbered north, turrs and hagdowns skimming our wake, our bow wave white, sails snapping in the uneven breeze. The dying sun lay off the larboard beam and lit the sea in a thousand jewels of light, broken only by the long swell that rose and fell between ship and shore. I watched as Skerries Bight and Small Point slipped past and Sugar Loaf Head loomed on our quarter. The ship's bell had just sounded the half-hour when I heard a low voice from near at hand. I turned to see the boatswain standing on the gangway, his grey head ducking in salute. He cast a wary eye at the captain's back and asked if the gunroom might have the pleasure of my company. My watch on deck was hours away and I accepted most happily, for Frost and the other warrant officers had at times invited me to their mess for a turn at cards or to share a bottle. It was kind of them, though I knew it was done out of misguided pity.

The reason for their sympathy had its origins in my interruption of service on board the *Guernsey*. In the previous winter I had spent some months ashore at Portsmouth, recovering from the scurvy. Until then, I'd served as the ship's signal officer, a busy enough post and one that I confess to having enjoyed for the stimulation it offered. On my return to duty, I had hopes of taking up where I'd left off, but found instead that a midshipman of family and influence had been given my place. I was therefore assigned responsibility for the aft larboard guns and the men who were quartered there.

I was disappointed, to be sure, but the change of circumstance did not bother me greatly. I made the most of my new duties and learned all that I could about the science of gunnery. I was equally resigned to the knowledge that things were unlikely to change in the near future. Favour and promotion were scarce in times of peace and scarcer still for those who had no one to hasten their preferment. However, a contrary view prevailed in the gunroom. There, the warrant officers were of the opinion that I had been most grievously wronged. They felt it augured ill for my chances of promotion, when in fact I had already come to terms with that reality. I would scarcely have given the matter another thought but they considered it an insult—if not an outrage—and one that ought to be addressed by the highest authority. That afternoon, as I sat to a glass of sugared rum with Frost and Simeon Bolger, the ship's gunner, the topic was broached once more.

"And have ye spoken to Mister Cartwright, sir?" Bolger asked. His elbows took up much of the space on the little table between us.

"I have not," I replied. "And I do not foresee doing so." My reply was always the same and invariably caused the gunner to shake his bald head in frustration.

"Tisn't fair, sir. Tisn't fair at all." He clamped his pipe between two of the few teeth he possessed and fixed me with a narrowed eye. Bolger had sailed with me on the old *Northum-*

berland and felt it his due to take small liberties, which I neither encouraged nor dissuaded. Lately he'd been pressing me to have the first lieutenant intervene on my behalf.

"Aye," Frost joined in. "An injustice is what it is. An injustice what should be put to rights." He shook his head as well, wagging the grey pigtail that fell halfway to his waist. His small eyes watched me from under a forehead that was hatched with scars and wrinkles. "Not right, sir," he muttered. "Not right in the least." I sipped my rum and did nothing to encourage them.

The gunner scratched his prominent jaw, embedded blue grains of gunpowder visible beneath the stubble. His face and hands were peppered with the marks of countless ignitions, the tattoos of his profession. "And why would ye not talk to Mister Cartwright, sir?" Bolger persisted.

I assumed a patient expression and replied, "My superiors have seen fit to put me at other quarters, Mister Bolger. It is not my place, nor that of anyone else"—I gave them both a meaningful look—"to question that decision."

The two men exchanged a glance and fixed me in their gaze. "Do ye think, sir," the gunner asked, "that it might have to do with something in particular?" Before I could answer, he added: "Not meaning yer knowledge, sir. Oh, no! Why, I've known captains that haven't yer mastery of signals, nor of navigation nor making sail. Oh no, there be something more, sir. There be something what keeps ye from having what's rightfully yer due."

"Well, tis not his record o' service, now, is it?" the boatswain countered. I sat back and tried not to smile. When they referred to me in the third person, it was an artful hint that I should heed what they had to say.

"Nay, not his record of service," the other exclaimed. "Why, ye only need look at him. His face bears his history, with them scars from the Battle of Quiberon Bay."

My hand moved of its own accord to the cobweb of white lines that radiated outward from my left eye. Frost nodded and said, "Strong he is, too." He formed a fist with his gnarled right hand. "Not so much in body, being as skinny as the purser's cat, but in spirit, and as bold a sailor as any you'll see." The large fist landed on the table for emphasis.

"Aye," said Bolger, "so the answer lies elsewhere, I'll wager. Perhaps it got more to do with where a body is born or who a body knows."

Frost grunted his agreement.

"Perhaps it got to do with a body not being seen as a proper gentleman. What with being an orphan and all, with no family nor connections."

The ponderous boatswain shook his head and sighed. "Blocked from promotion by birth. Aye, tis a sad thing the old Navy is come to."

"A sad thing indeed, mate. A very sad thing."

I was about to speak in my own defence, assuming they'd finished their discourse on social inequity, when Frost suddenly piped: *"Birds of a feather will flock together, and so will pigs and swine. Rats and mice will have their choice and so will I have mine!"*

Impromptu recitations were a peculiarity of the boatswain. He was in the habit of bringing forth bits of doggerel verse, usually children's rhymes, to suit any occasion. While this was rarely subtle, it was often amusing and I decided to let him have the final word. The boatswain, sensing he'd made his point well enough, allowed the subject to drop. The same could not be said of the gunner, who was tapping his lower tooth with the stem of his pipe.

"What our Mister Squibb has need of," he said at length, "is a patron who might advance his interests. Or a senior officer who might grease the blocks fer a deserving young gentleman."

The boatswain slurped his rum and said nothing.

"Like our Cap'n Palliser, fer an instance," Bolger said. "Now, if Mister Squibb was to perform some service fer him, as a volunteer like, then the cap'n would no doubt be grateful and in his debt. Wouldn't that be so?"

Frost grunted once more in a manner that conveyed his agreement.

"Now what might that service be, I wonder?" the gunner mused. "If only there was some occasion—"

"By thunder, there might be one at that!" the boatswain exclaimed, though in so pat a manner that I suspected them of having rehearsed their lines.

"And what would that be?" Bolger asked, feigning surprise.

"Why, haven't the cap'n's steward been putting it about that we're going on to Fogo Island? And not just to meet the *Lark* and the *Tweed*, but to further Mister Palliser's plan o' finding the Red Indians? Ye must have heard, cause that steward can't stop his tongue. I don't know why the cap'n keeps him, I don't."

"The Red Indians, ye say? What's all this about?"

"Why, Mister Palliser thinks they'll all be killed off."

The exchange had by now caught my interest in spite of myself. I had heard many tales of the Red Indians as a boy in Trinity, though what I or anyone else actually knew of them amounted to very little. All I could say with certainty was that they were an elusive tribe that populated the interior wilderness and remote bays of the northeast coast. Like most people, I'd been led to believe that they rarely showed themselves except to attack or steal from our fishermen.

"And how would Mister Squibb go about getting the cap'n's gratitude, then?" Bolger asked.

"Why, Mister Palliser aims to send Lieutenant Cartwright into the forest to find the Red Indians. The steward says he wants to make a treaty with 'em."

The gunner rubbed his blue-flecked jaw. "So?"

"Well, the cap'n's not going to send Mister Cartwright off alone, now is he? He'll be wanting volunteers and if Mister Squibb was to step forward and acquit hisself, well, wouldn't the cap'n be indebted to him and give him his signal post?" He added, with a meaningful wink, "Or even a promotion?"

"By Christ, he might at that!" Bolger exclaimed. "Yes, he might at that."

I said nothing and concentrated on my rum while they tried to gauge my reaction. They would not have been able to tell but their little pantomime had impressed me very much, though not for the reason they'd intended. My curiosity was stirred not by the opportunity to advance my own interests, but by the rumour that Mr. Palliser would try to make peace with the Red Indians. If there were truth to the steward's gossip then I would certainly wish to be part of such a remarkable expedition. The warrant officers toyed with their cups and took pains to appear indifferent. I looked through the open gunport and saw, far across the water, the cliffs of Cape St. Francis. Only then did I realize that the ship was no longer making way. The fitful westerly had died with our conversation and the *Guernsey*, like my two companions, had lapsed into an unusual silence.

Hugh Palliser

I am damned if I know how news travels so quickly aboard this vessel. Not an hour has passed since I informed Lieutenant Cartwright of my plan and already three people have come to my cabin door, asking to be sent on this expedition. I know it is impossible to keep anything from the ears of four hundred men so tightly packed on board a ship, but I should not be surprised if the Red Indians themselves have heard of my scheme.

The first of my visitors was Mr. George Cartwright, who is with us as the guest of his brother John. I judge him to be a most active and enterprising gentleman and so his request comes as no surprise. As an officer of the 37th Foot, he saw much action in the last war and his experience may prove useful. My only reservation lies in his fondness for killing things. When he is not shooting he is talking of shooting, and woe betide the bird, beast or fish that falls within his sights.

No sooner had I returned to my dinner than another knock came to the door, this time from Mr. Squibb, my third lieutenant. He, too, had heard of my plan and was asking to be included in the party. I have no objection, I suppose, considering that he has served under Hawke and Colville and has favourable letters from both. Indeed, I have no reason to complain of his conduct on board the *Guernsey* either, unlike that of my other lieutenant, the insufferable Mr. Tench. Squibb may be somewhat bookish for my taste but I believe he will serve the purpose well enough and may even prove a level head when one is needed.

My third caller was more of a surprise, I will admit. The last person I expected to see was the Reverend Neville Stow. Our ship's chaplain has always struck me as a retiring individual, more suited to prayer and sermonizing than battling man and nature. I find him a peculiar sort, all elbows and knees and a great deal of nasal hee-hawing and snorting, much in the manner of a mule. I do him an injustice, no doubt, but he has the manner of a man who is far too secure in his own convictions. I am more at ease with those who would keep an open mind, particularly on so delicate a subject as the Red Indians.

Still, the Reverend made a convincing case for being included, as the poor Indians are no doubt in need of Christian teaching. He also pointed out, somewhat impertinently I may say, that I have allowed the Moravian missionaries to go among the war-like Esquimaux of Labrador. That is true enough, though Jens Haven and his people have had little success thus far. In fact, I would not be surprised to learn that they had met an untimely end in that God-forsaken place. All the same, I have decided to allow Reverend Stow to accompany the expedition, so long as he does not prove a hindrance to its progress or its purpose.

The matter of the Red Indians has been much upon my mind of late. Lieutenant Cartwright tells me that he has also been preoccupied with the subject, as would any person with even a trace of humanity. Cartwright's principles may extend a touch too far, however. I have heard him expounding upon the need for reform in areas where the dog is best left sleeping. He openly advocates the abolition of Negro slavery, even in the company of men who own great estates in the Indies. And he is never shy to express his view that the American colonies should not be taxed to pay for the last war with France. These are nearly seditious sentiments but he is a competent officer who has risen quickly and shall go further still, if he learns to keep his mouth shut.

The same cannot be said of Mr. Tench, however. He is a man well accustomed to keeping his mouth shut when it comes to his own dealings, though he is vocal enough in opposing my plan to pursue peace with the Red Indians. He claims it is far too late and they will not be moved, and in any event it is a venture with little return. I suspect there is a reason for his opinion, but like so many things about the man, it is deeply hidden.

As I was saying, the poor savages of this island have been on my mind of late, their plight having been ignored for much too long. I am now bound and determined to change the course of their unfortunate history and I believe that an effort to make peace with them will prove to be the turning point. Indeed, it will be the first time that an offer of the King's protection has ever been extended to them. There is much to be gained in this endeavour, not least the salvation of their heathen souls and the assurance of their loyalty to the Crown.

Another advantage, which appeals to the merchants of the island, is that they may be enticed to trade with us. These men are eager for new supplies of furs from the interior in exchange for things the Indians require or for which they may develop a taste. It has been suggested that rum is a suitable commodity, it being the principal item of trade in Canada, where it is in great demand among the natives. There is certainly no lack of that substance here, as it is brought from the Jamaicas in return for salted cod to feed the slaves. But I believe the question may deserve further consideration.

How the Red Indians came to be reduced to their present state is another vexing matter. There can be no doubt that our increased presence on the northeast coast has affected them, for they have lost territory that has traditionally yielded their food. Matters have not been aided in the least by those who have opened up this new frontier. They are a wild, ungovernable people and in some respects, as savage and barbarous as the Indians themselves. They have responded to the Indians' pilfering with the greatest violence and God alone knows how many they have killed in years past, or how many will be killed in years to come if an end is not put to the practice at once.

I have no means of knowing their truth but reports have reached me of men travelling into the forest for the sole purpose of hunting and killing these miserable creatures. They reason that if the Red Indians are destroyed, the pilfering will end, as I am sure it will, but at what cost? Wholesale murder to preserve a few traps and nets? If I do not act now, I am certain that the English nation, like the Spanish, may soon bear the indelible reproach of having destroyed an entire race of people.

Another factor that enters into my consideration is the presence of the French in the area, along with their allies, the Mickmack Indians. I am convinced that they are carrying on a clandestine trade in furs when they have no rights to do so under the Treaty of Paris. The Mickmacks are moving ever deeper into the island in search of those furs, and confrontations with the Red Indians are inevitable, if not already taking place. I shudder at the outcome of such a conflict, when the French have armed their allies with muskets and their adversaries have nothing more than spears and arrows. The red man is pressed on all sides, it seems, and his only hope may lie in the success of our expedition.

I am also continuing my efforts on the political front. For some time I have been petitioning the Colonial Office for authority to issue a proclamation, the wording of which I have already drafted. It reads thus: "Whereas it has been represented to the King that his subjects residing in the island of Newfoundland, instead of cultivating a friendly intercourse with the savages inhabiting that island, do treat the savages with the greatest inhumanity and frequently destroy them without the least provocation or remorse. In order, therefore, to put a stop to these atrocities and to bring the perpetrators of such crimes to justice, it is His Majesty's royal will and pleasure to express his abhorrence of these acts and to enjoin his subjects to live in amity and brotherly kindness with the natives of the island. He

Derek Yetman

also requires and commands that all magistrates and officers use their utmost diligence to discover and apprehend those persons who may be guilty of murdering the Indians, that such offenders may be sent to England to be tried for their crimes."

Of course, I cannot say when this edict will be approved and I am not likely to hold my water until it is. Instead, I have another device in mind that may bring about the object of peace more quickly than any other. After much reflection, I have decided that it would be in the interest of all concerned if we were to capture a Red Indian and impress upon him or her our peaceful intentions. I have instructed my captains to make this known to all the fishermen and planters along the coast, and to inform them that a reward of £50 is offered to any man who can deliver such a captive.

I have employed this strategy already in the case of the Esquimaux. A woman named Mikak was captured near Fort York last season and I have sent her and two children to England. There they will learn the King's English and return to their people with assurances of our Christian intent. I am resolved to follow a similar course with the Red Indians, as this may be the only means to a lasting peace.

Jonah Squibb

It was an event that had no equal, either before or after, in the logs and lore of the Newfoundland station. The *Guernsey* lay becalmed for two days off Cape St. Francis and the captain himself was at a loss to explain it or do anything about it. He grew increasingly vexed as the day for our rendezvous with the *Liverpool* came and went, and all manner of things were attempted at his orders, including towing and warping ourselves in every direction in search of a breath of air. The sails were kept wetted night and day on the chance of drawing a breeze, however faint. As a last resort the sailors even fell to whistling. Others were stationed in the tops at all hours, watching for the slightest ripple on the water. If one were seen, imagined or not, the boats were manned and off we rowed to catch it. And to add to our frustration, the sun was uncommonly hot throughout. The men suffered a great deal at the oars and capstan, and one or two fell senseless from the rigging.

It was all in vain, of course, for the wind returned in its own good time. Henry Fielding summed it up quite nicely, I thought, when he wrote in his *Journal* that "the most absolute power of a captain of a ship is very contemptible in the wind's eye." On the evening of the seventeenth it began as little more than a whisper, a vague hint of movement in the air. I detected it on the quarterdeck at the same instant as the men aloft. It took a moment to discern its direction but I soon judged it to be easterly. Our bow was then pointed in that direction and at my word the longboat quickly brought the ship about, the commotion bringing Lieutenant Cartwright on deck. The boat cast off her hawser and fell alongside to be hoisted in, even as I ordered more buckets of water aloft to wet the sails.

"What is it, Mister Squibb?" he asked. "Is it a breeze?"

"Aye, sir," I replied. "And a promising one, I think."

"You there," the lieutenant said to a midshipman who was standing nearby. "Inform the captain that we have a wind. And where is Frost? Where the devil is that bo'sun?"

"On the booms, sir," I said, "having the longboat secured." I had observed over the course of our association that Mr. Cartwright was inclined to be excitable, particularly when time was of the essence. The normally composed features of his well-bred face became animated, his lips pursing and puckering and the nostrils of his thin nose flaring like the wings of a skate.

"Mister Frost!" he called, the colour rising in his cheeks. The boatswain looked up from his task and shielded his eyes against the lowering sun. "All hands to the halyards. Be ready to square and trim at my command. We'll catch what we can of this infant's breath."

"Aye, aye, sir." The boatswain turned and issued his orders to the waiting watch. They hopped at his command—as well they might if they had any regard for the skin on their backs. Our Frost was not a man to be ignored when he required something done at once. He ruled his domain with a heart that was two parts stone and one part fatherly tyranny, and his manner had long ago earned him the nickname of "Hard" Frost. Even his mates, the petty officers who worked under him, regarded the boatswain with a wary eye when things were not on an even keel.

Captain Palliser came on deck in his shirtsleeves, accompanied by the chaplain, and looked up at the sagging canvas. He said nothing as he waited for the evidence. A minute later, just as I was beginning to doubt it myself, the sails began to flutter and billow. Seven bells were struck in the second dogwatch and the captain remained where he was, the Reverend Stow beside him and mimicking his posture. I was guessing that the chaplain had no idea of what he was looking at, when suddenly the main royal filled with a crack, followed by the topgallant. The crew on deck and in the shrouds gave a spontaneous cheer and a shadow of approval crept across the captain's face. Reverend Stow, a fawning look upon his horsy countenance, congratulated Mr. Palliser with the enthusiasm of one who'd witnessed the greatest of naval victories.

For the rest of that evening we were favoured with a light easterly of four or five knots. Just after midnight, early in the middle watch, we cleared the northern tip of Baccalieu Island. We had the wind on our beam for the most part, though we tacked and sailed close-hauled from time to time to correct our shoreward drift. At dawn on the following day, I made Cape Bonavista in the circle of my glass with the wind rising steadily and veering sharply to the west. I sensed a blow approaching and was not far wrong, for soon the swell increased and dark clouds gathered on the northern horizon.

The weather was of little concern on the quarterdeck, as we would soon be within the harbour and reasonably sheltered. Bonavista was not an ideal sanctuary for a ship of the line but it would serve if the need arose. I had been to the place several times as a boy and as we rounded Green Island, I saw the flakes that ringed the treeless plain below the cape. This was no longer the most northerly settlement on the coast but it was still the centre of the area's prosperous fishery. I was thinking of old John Cabot, who was said to have sighted land here centuries before, when I realized that the tall masts of the *Liverpool* were nowhere to be seen. The rising wind quickly brought us to within half a league of shore and our sails were being reefed when I observed a boat emerging from the inner harbour. It was under a press of sail and heading for the *Guernsey*, and making heavy weather of it in the short swell. I summoned the gunner and conferred with him briefly before informing Mr. Cartwright of the vessel's approach. He joined me at the rail with his tricorn hat in one hand and the remains of his breakfast in the other.

"What do you make of it, Mister Squibb?" he asked through a mouthful of bread.

I studied the boat through my glass. "She may have a message for us, sir. I can see no other reason to sail in the teeth of a coming gale."

The lieutenant grunted and watched our visitor, the wind snatching at his wig. "What the devil is it, do you think?" he asked. "I thought a sloop, but I'm damned if it doesn't look more like a fishing shallop."

He was perfectly correct, as the vessel might have been taken for either. It was a peculiar little craft of some forty feet in length, with a single mast instead of the ketch-rigged short main and mizzen that would normally equip a shallop. But she did have the hull of a Newfoundland boat, with an open hold for fish, although she'd been fitted with a decked stern and forecastle in the manner of a sloop. She carried a mainsail, fore staysail and jib, and oddly enough a bare yard was slung from her mainmast, signifying the ability to carry a topsail as well. The most surprising feature of her appearance, however, was the fact that she was armed.

When I remarked as much to the lieutenant he exclaimed, "What!" and put the glass to his eye. "I think that Captain Palliser should—"

"What the devil is this, Mister Cartwright?" The lieutenant flinched at the sound of the captain's voice. "Why was I not informed of this vessel's approach?" He was standing immediately behind us, the foppish chaplain at his side.

"My apologies, sir," the lieutenant replied. "We were just attempting to discern the vessel's character before—"

"Yes, yes," the captain said, impatiently relieving him of the glass. "Your watch is it, Mister Squibb? What do you make of her, then?"

I avoided Mr. Cartwright's eye and said, "Four swivel guns, sir. One pounders, I should say, and the gunwales newly cut to accommodate them."

"And what sort of vessel is she?"

"A large fishing shallop, sir. Sloop-rigged fore and aft. In a manner of speaking."

Mr. Palliser snorted his disapproval that boats should be rigged so contrary to convention. "You know your duty, Mister Squibb. What measures have you taken?"

"I have instructed Mister Bolger to ready a pair of eighteens, sir."

"Very good, young sir. Well done, indeed. Speak to her master and report to me, Mister Cartwright. Armed, is she? We'll see about this."

The captain limped off to his cabin with the chaplain at his heels, leaving Mr. Cartwright and myself in awkward silence. The lieutenant's face, rarely a study in composure, was as rigid as the figurehead that graced our bow. The shallop made her way to the shelter of our lee with the muzzles of our guns following her approach.

"The boat ahoy!" Mr. Cartwright sang across the water. "Name your vessel."

A sailor on the tiny forecastle gave him a puzzled look. "Can't tell ye, sir," he replied, "seein' as how she got no name."

The lieutenant's nostrils flared and he tried again. "Who are you and what is your business?" A seaman snickered in the mizzen shrouds above us but when I looked I was met with sober faces.

"We's off the *Liverpool*," the man called. "This here is her hired boat. The cap'n left us behind to tell ye he's sailed for the Change Islands."

"The Change Islands!" Mr. Cartwright exclaimed. "He was supposed to wait here for Captain Palliser."

"Aye, sir," the man shouted against the wind, "only he heard of a French brig-o'-war bein' seen there. He thought it best to go straight away."

The other two men in the shallop had by this time reduced her sail and the boat was beginning to roll in the swell. The first lieutenant seemed lost in thought and so I shouted, "Come alongside and make your report."

"Aye, aye, sir," was the reluctant reply and the man at the

tiller steered towards us under staysail alone. We soon learned that the sailor who'd done the talking was a petty officer named Grimes. He smelled of rum and a sour stomach and was taken aside to be questioned by Lieutenant Cartwright. I was left in charge of the quarterdeck and ordered the gun crews to stand down and likewise the marines, who were sighting their muskets on the two nervous men in the shallop.

Mr. Cartwright made his report to the captain, after which I was summoned to the cabin. What sounded like a heated conversation ended as I entered the dayroom, where the three senior officers of the ship were gathered. "Ah, Mr. Squibb," the captain said. "We have a change of plan. I want you to equip the shallop, or sloop or whatever the devil it may be, for a cruise of one month. You know what is needed, I am sure."

"How many crew shall I provision for, sir?"

The captain glanced at the first lieutenant. "Eight, I should think. Yes, there's the three men from the *Liverpool*, Revered Stow, Lieutenant Cartwright, Mister George Cartwright and Mister Cartwright's servant. And yourself, of course."

Lieutenant Cartwright, his face somewhat flushed, turned to the captain and said, "If you will excuse me, sir, I have much to attend to."

"Yes, yes. Of course."

As he left the cabin, Lieutenant Tench, who had been looking on with a frown on his pallid face and a distinct air of disapproval, cleared his throat. "With the greatest respect, sir, I must urge—"

"Enough, sir!" The captain's firm voice was pitched somewhat loud. Tench's lips tightened but the frown remained.

I hesitated, wondering whether I should ask our destination, when the captain supplied the answer for me: "I am taking the *Guernsey* to Fogo immediately. Lieutenant Cartwright will take command of the shallop and will follow me tomorrow. If he does not find me there, he will carry on with his orders to establish contact with the Red Indians."

On hearing this, I could barely contain a smile—I was to be included in the expedition after all! I kept a serious face as

Mr. Palliser continued: "In the event that I am not at Fogo, Mister Cartwright will seek out a planter there named John Cousens. He knows the area as well as any man and can provide advice on how to proceed. I am told he even has a Red Indian in his employ. His knowledge should be most valuable."

The captain limped to his writing chair and eased into it with a sigh. "Now then, Mister Squibb. When you have finished provisioning the vessel, I want you to take a watering party ashore. And while you are there, look in on a midshipman from the *Liverpool*, who is quartered at the surgeon's house. The petty officer says that he is quite ill. Of course, he may be dead by now, in which case you must see him properly buried."

"Yes, sir. And captain?"

"Yes?"

"The swivel guns in the shallop, sir—I assume they came from the *Liverpool*'s quarterdeck?"

"Yes, I suppose they did. What of it?"

"Shall I have the gunner look them over, sir? To ensure they're properly mounted and have enough powder and shot?" From the corner of my eye I saw Tench's pale, disapproving face turn to me.

"Yes, Mister Squibb. You may."

"And the shallop's rigging, sir. Perhaps the boatswain could see that everything is in order?"

"Of course, of course."

"And I should point out that she has no boat, sir. May I take our spare jolly boat in tow?"

"Indeed you may. Sound thinking, Mister Squibb. Very sound indeed."

"Thank you, sir." I withdrew from the room under two very different sets of eyes, one quite approving and the other as cold as a Newfoundland winter.

Hugh Palliser

Damn my eyes if it isn't the *Valeur* again! Damn them if it isn't. That boat has been the gall of my existence since I became governor and still the French persist in testing the limits of my patience. But this time they have gone too far. I will tolerate no more of this posturing and tomfoolery. Lurking around the Change Islands, are they? Not for long, I can promise you. The captains of the *Liverpool*, *Lark* and *Tweed* know the terms of our treaty with France. Any armed French vessel on this coast will be boarded and its officers arrested, and my ships may use what force they require. I shall soon put a stop to their excursions in that damnable brigantine. Even if I have to send it to the bottom.

Oh Lord, the pain I have today! There is weather coming, I can swear to that. Thunderheads in the northeast and the wind and swell nearly doubling in the past two hours. And this blasted leg of mine—I need to put it up on something. There, that's better, though I know the pain will be unbearable before the day is out. What was I saying? Oh yes. Blister my tripes but the French have more swagger than common sense. Imagine cruising English waters with that little *Valeur*, when they know there are four English ships-of-war about. And to what end? To harass a few poor fishermen? Or more likely, to remind us that the French shore begins at Cape Bonavista. Which is what the treaty says, though the reality is quite different.

This all began in 1763, at the end of the Seven Years' War, when France was obliged to recognize our sovereignty over Newfoundland. In return, they were permitted to catch and dry fish between Cape Bonavista and Cape Riche, which is on the northern half of the island's west coast. But they were not content with that and struck upon a clever scheme to claim that Cape Riche was actually Cape Ray, at the southern extremity of the west coast. I ask you, has there ever been a more transparent fraud? They even said they possessed the maps to prove it! Imagine, if you will, an error of nearly three degrees north latitude, giving France the entire west coast of the colony.

Well, if that was their game, then we were equal to it. If they intended to twist the terms of the treaty, then what was to stop our own people from moving into the coves and harbours north of Cape Bonavista? That is exactly the case at present and the French have threatened war unless their rights to the shore are upheld. They even sent a naval squadron to back their demands a few years ago, which kept my hands full, I can tell you. England relented in the end and both sides accepted the original boundaries, though my orders say nothing about stopping the expansion of English enterprise along the northeast coast. My instructions are merely to prevent our people from interfering with the French fishery.

All of this has enraged France, of course, and given their naval officers a *cause célèbre*. In my opinion, it all comes down to a matter of interpretation. The treaty states that France shall have use of the shore to fish but there is nothing to specifically exclude the English. Tit for tat is what I call it, after their Cape Riche contrivance. Ah, it's a complicated enough business without them making it a point of honour. No doubt this little show with the *Valeur* is in reply to that unfortunate incident at Toulinguet last month. A French captain named Delarue was forced off his fishing room and now there is news that our people have burnt French premises at Quirpon as well. I suppose I shall have to write Governor d'Angeac at St. Pierre again, for all the good it will do. He will complain about our fishermen and say that he knows nothing of the *Valeur*'s actions, and then he will wash his hands of the matter.

Mary and Joseph, how I wish the surgeon had taken off this leg when he had the chance. I have cursed him these twenty years for not doing so. May the Lord give me strength, for I shall have need of it, between this cursed weather and these damnable Frenchmen. Perhaps if I use this pillow, just so ...

Jonah Squibb

   Evening was upon us before the shallop was fully loaded with our sacks and kegs of provisions. From the *Guernsey*'s stores I had drawn flour, cheese, dried peas, butter, dried plums, ship's biscuit and salted beef and pork. All we lacked was fresh meat, but the purser refused to give me so much as a small goat. He said that we would find what we needed in the settlements along the coast. I replied that there were no settlements on the coast—only fishing stations that had no livestock. His answer was that there would be plenty of game in the wild. This was true enough, although I feigned ignorance and argued until he gave me extra powder and shot for the small arms to be put on board. To all of this I added our empty water barrels, a box of tobacco leaf, a small cask of wine and another of Jamaica rum.

  During this time, Lieutenant Cartwright occupied himself in getting charts and instruments from the ship's master. From the sound of their discussion, the man was none too happy to part with his precious items. Bolger had come on board to make an inspection of the guns and was good enough to stay and supervise the three *Liverpool*s in stowing the barrels. Frost was also aboard, with Greening, and they went aloft to inspect our mast and rigging. At about nine o'clock, with less than an hour of daylight remaining, Lieutenant Cartwright, his brother, his brother's servant and Reverend Stow came into the boat to look it over. My own sea chest had been shifted already and, with the exception of receiving the gentlemen's baggage, all was in order. The only complaint came from the chaplain, who was not enamoured of the strong smell of fish that hung over the shallop.

The lieutenant had decided that we would go ashore before dark to attend to the water and the ailing midshipman. We would spend the night in the harbour before sailing in the *Guernsey*'s wake in the morning. The boatswain being nearly finished his inspection, Lieutenant Cartwright suggested that we take the craft on a short cruise to test her sails before we parted company. Neither the boatswain nor I would acknowledge the soundness of his idea, given the strength of the wind, but he was determined to follow it through. In spite of the chaplain's protests, we were ordered to cast off from the lee of the *Guernsey* without delay.

The previously strong wind had risen a good deal while our vessel was being loaded. As soon as we left the protection of the ship's hull, we found ourselves in a gale that was rapidly approaching a storm. The shallop was well founded and built to carry a great weight of fish in a heavy sea, and she rode the swells handily enough under reefed main and staysail. With me at the helm, she came within a few points of the wind on the starboard tack before Lieutenant Cartwright ordered me to bear away. This put us broadside to the swell for a few moments, which was enough to turn Reverend Stow a deathly pale from either sickness or fright. A few nasty-looking waves, whipped up by the wind at the crest of a swell, gave us a wetting and I thought the poor chaplain would expire on the spot. He fell against the gunwale, throwing his arms around the barrel of a swivel gun, and there he stayed.

Events took a turn for the worse a moment later. The shallop had fallen off the wind and we were scarcely on a broad reach when the mainsail split with a crack as loud as a musket shot. Everyone but Reverend Stow looked up at the torn canvas, Frost swearing under his breath before ordering the rag hauled down. This was exactly the sort of calamity I'd feared and which can happen when sailing an unproven boat in a gathering storm. At Mister Cartwright's command I put the tiller over and pointed us for the *Guernsey*, even as I ordered the staysail loosened in order to scud with the wind astern.

It was here that a second calamity befell us. The staysail earring let go in a powerful gust, leaving the sail flapping like a sheet on a washline. The hands rushed to gather it in before Frost stopped them in their tracks with a barked order to unbend the jibsail. He was perfectly correct in this, of course, as a fluttering staysail was the least of our worries. We were now without control of the vessel and therefore at the mercy of the elements, which were quick to put us broadside to the wind and swell. The men jumped to the boatswain's command, but to my wonder Lieutenant Cartwright belayed the order, calling instead for the topsail. This in itself was not a poor decision, as a closely reefed topsail will serve as well as a jib in a pinch. But it did mean the loss of valuable time. The men had already begun to loosen the jib's lashing and now had to abandon the task.

Reverend Stow was not taking the excitement well. His face betrayed his terror at our situation and he clung to the gun as though it were something that would not drag him to the bottom the instant we broke apart. Our other gentleman, Mr. George Cartwright, was standing amidships with his hand on a shroud for balance. In profile he looked very much like his brother, except his smiling face displayed his ignorance of the danger we were in.

By now we were taking the brunt of the wind's fury and rolling like a puncheon in the mountainous swell. Frost was standing next to me, his face as dark as the lowering sky. He nodded in the direction of Reverend Stow and the two Cartwrights, and above the strumming and whistling of the wind in the rigging, I heard him say: "*Three wise men of Gotham went to sea in a bowl; if the bowl had been stronger, my poem would've been longer!*"

We drifted past the high stern of the *Guernsey*, where no

particular attention was being paid to us, and were driving broadside for the rocks at the mouth of Bonavista Harbour. Greening and the three *Liverpool*s worked like demons and were finally able to set the small topsail. It filled immediately, and our bow swung away from the wind just as an enormous roller came under our stern. The shallop rose as if it were no more than a chip of wood and for an instant I felt the rudder come free of the water. We were lifted and propelled at the same time, and we felt a profound sense of helplessness as the wave hurled us deeper into the harbour. At that moment, above the roar of the tempest, I heard the voice of the chaplain wailing, "How vast is thy sea, O Lord, and how small is my boat!"

It was as close a thing as ever I'd witnessed, much less experienced. If the wind had been another point northerly the sea would have careened us onto our beam ends and into the rocks. The small topsail had provided some control but I still had the tiller hard fast under my arm, trying to avoid the rocky lee shore. I managed to veer us off to windward before a strong gust put our starboard gunwale under, snapping a line and sending two kegs over the side.

In another breath or two we were safe and sound, though in a fine pickle all the same. The *Guernsey* was due to sail at any moment and here we were with her gunner and boatswain, plus young Greening, on board the shallop. To make matters worse, we could not take the boat back out, owing to the strength and direction of the wind and the lack of room to tack in the harbour mouth. Mr. Cartwright was thoroughly nettled, as was the chaplain, who had let go of the gun and was now demanding to be returned to the ship.

I knew, as did the warrant officers, that we would not be going near the *Guernsey* anytime soon. Captain Palliser could not wait for the weather to improve even if he had a mind to do so. The ship's bowers were barely holding her now and he would not ride the worsening storm at anchor. A parted cable would mean being driven ashore in the middle of the night and no captain would take that risk for want of two or three men, however useful they might be to his vessel.

I gave the tiller to Frost and clambered over the cargo to the first lieutenant, intending to tell him as much. But before I could speak, I heard him tell his brother and Reverend Stow that we were as good as stranded in the harbour. We were unlikely to see the *Guernsey* before Fogo, he said, if indeed then. I was pleased that he had a full appreciation of our situation, since he was largely to blame for it. His brother George merely shrugged at the news, his experience in the army having no doubt accustomed him to sudden changes of plan. The chaplain was not quite so accepting and griped loudly at the suggestion that he would have to make do with nothing more than the clothes on his back. He was a pitiful, if not a comic sight, with his mournful face and dripping wig. He was no soldier and even less a sailor and I could not help but wonder why he'd volunteered for this voyage.

To add to the chaplain's misery, it began to rain as we were securing the errant barrels and repacking our kegs. In short order it was coming on with a fury. I instructed the boatswain to rig canopies from the damaged sails while the seamen took to the sweeps and rowed us across the harbour. We soon came alongside a stage where two splitters, their canvas aprons and boots covered in blood and gurry, left the shelter of a storeroom and tied us fast. It was a prosperous fishing room with a good many flakes and stores and a substantial house in a nearby field. The men said it was owned by Mr. Joseph White and managed by his agent, Thomas Street. If Reverend Stow had found the smell of our boat offensive, I could only imagine what he thought of this place. The stench of fish would have stopped a town clock.

It was now coming on dark and Mr. Cartwright instructed me to go to the house of the local surgeon, that I might learn the condition of the sick midshipman from the *Liverpool*. I took one of the frigate's seamen with me as a guide and we crossed the harbour in the jolly boat, landing near a wooden shack that looked in danger of falling over in the wind. I knocked and stood for a time in the rain before a door of rough planks was unlatched and an untidy woman peered out at me. I told her my business and she admitted me reluctantly, insisting that my guide remain outside. This struck me as most inhospitable, until I remembered that the *Liverpool* sailors had been here for two weeks without an officer. They had probably raised the devil in that time.

My eyes began to water as soon as I stepped inside, the air being thick with smoke from a crude chimney of loose, flat stones. The surgeon was not at home, the woman said, but she would show me to the young gentleman. I followed her across the flagstone floor and into a tiny coffin of a room, where a thin form lay on its side, the face obscured beneath a counterpane. By the glow of her lamp, I saw the moisture and mildew on the walls and the scurrying vermin that disappeared into cracks and shadows.

"How long has he been ill?" I asked.

She looked down at the slight figure and shrugged. "Don't rightly know. 'E were bought 'ere nearly a fortnight past and 'e were sick when 'e come."

"And what is the nature of his illness?"

"Master says 'e got da scurvy."

I nodded, not at all surprised that the most common affliction of the Navy had struck this young man down. During my own recovery, I had read a treatise on the disease that was newly written by a surgeon named Lind. He seemed to think that oranges and lemons were an effective cure, which I suppose was well and good if you fell ill in the Mediterranean.

"What treatments has the surgeon applied?" I asked.

The woman shrugged. "Diff'rent ones. First 'e covered 'im up to 'is neck in soil but after a few days da sores got worse, like. Then 'e give 'im doses o' tarwater, only 'e couldn't keep it down. Lately 'e been bleedin' 'im every few hours."

I had experienced all of these so-called remedies and knew of none that was worth the suffering endured by the patient. "Anything more?" I asked.

She took down a tiny bowl from a nearby shelf. "Just dis med'cine." I lifted the thimble of reddish brown powder to my nose and recoiled at the pungently bitter smell.

The Beothuk Expedition

"What is the boy's name?" I asked, returning the bowl and stepping closer to the bed. I took hold of the sheet and her reply came as I drew it back. I cannot say if it was the name in my ear or the face before me that gave me such a shock.

John Cartwright

It was a close thing with that confounded shallop, I have to say. Of course, had the boatswain not issued orders contrary to my wishes, we would have weathered the affair quite nicely. Valuable time was lost in sending the hands to the jibsail first, when that was clearly not my intention. But there is no harm done, other than the addition of three men to my crew and the lack of our baggage. I am certain that we shall prosper all the same, provided the boatswain remembers his place on my vessel.

The *Guernsey* has now parted company, leaving me to my own resources until we reach Fogo Island. I have decided that, if the ship is not there when we arrive, we shall provision as best we can and set a course for the Bay of Exploits. Mr. Palliser has determined that Man of War Cove, on the southern end of Fogo Island, will be our alternate rendezvous in a fortnight from now. In the meantime, I have made it known to all and sundry at Bonavista that a reward is offered for a captive Red Indian. Our host, Mr. Street, seems to have some reservation on this. He has said little, however, other than to note that a great many ruffians have passed through the town this summer, bound for the fishing stations of the northeast coast.

Mr. Street informs me as well that there are many criminal charges waiting to be heard there. I have not the least knowledge of these cases but I can easily imagine the offences involved. They will include assault, theft, wanton damage to property and so on, and no doubt the greater part of it will be down to the immoderate consumption of spirits. Many of those brought before the court will also be of the Irish race. This I know from experience. They will be young men for the most past, shipped to Newfoundland because their families or parishes were unable to support them at home. Here they are known as White Boys, though few of them have actual ties to that rebel cause. They may sympathize with it and why should they not? English landlords have been turning them off their tenant farms and crofts for years, evicting them with no compensation, few skills and even fewer prospects.

Reverend Balfour at Trinity has informed the governor that his parish has been the scene of many outrages, where from want and necessity the Irish riot frequently. The English settlers have been forced to draw together for their own protection and no man will accept the duties of constable, for fear of his life. Many of these Irish routinely die of starvation and exposure in winter. I myself have arrested individuals for manslaughter that was brought on by desperation and fuelled by intoxicating spirits. Only last year, a young woman named Hannah Barrett was tormented by a mob of these fellows and run off a cliff to her death. The situation has not improved a year hence, for recently I've heard that a gang of scoundrels has been terrorizing Trinity once more. As surrogate magistrate, I have no time to deal with them now but I shall certainly clip their wings on my return.

Even the Irish who have employment here are no better off, it seems. Their employers will cheat them and abuse them given half the chance, and they do not help themselves with their weakness for drink. Captain Palliser has had occasion to reprimand certain English merchants for paying their servants with rum instead of wages. Unable to buy their passage home at the season's end, these servants are abandoned to debauchery and wickedness for six months of the year. They become perfect strangers to all government, religion and good order.

Derek Yetman

One of the most notorious merchants for this is Andrew Pinson, an agent of John Noble at Toulinguet. The governor has reprimanded him repeatedly for landing his crews at St. John's in the fall and paying them entirely in spirits. While he and his methods are condemned by us, his business fellows love him even less, owing to his attempts at monopolizing the fur and salmon trade on this coast. Pinson, I am bound to say, is the epitome of all that is wrong with this place, for the man is Greed itself.

By contrast, it has been most gratifying to serve under an individual as enlightened as Captain Palliser. We are of the same mind in believing that the lower classes do not have to be kept poor in order to be kept industrious. We are part of the new order, he and I: compassionate, yet firm and consistent in administering justice to the lower ranks of society. I recall our very first conversation, on whether God had established our social system, and whether poverty, pain and death are part of the mystery of Creation. We are both inclined to think it is so, though we shall never shrink from appeasing human suffering where we find it.

Suffering is a word that I have heard frequently of late. The Reverend Stow is most insistent that we catch up with the *Guernsey* to prevent our own suffering. Of course, I suspect that our ecclesiastical friend is more concerned with his personal comfort than with any true suffering on the part of the crew. The word has also been used by Mr. Squibb, in connection with a midshipman who was left here by the *Liverpool*. He seems to think the boy will suffer and die if he is left in the care of a former naval surgeon. These surgeons may be crude in their methods, I will admit, but it would be impossible to take a bedridden man on an expedition such as this. Still, our young Mr. Squibb can be most persistent, a distasteful quality that I have noted in him. But Mr. Palliser is not here to favour him now, and so he shall have to obey my orders on the subject. We are overcrowded as it is and our provisions were meant for eight men, not eleven and certainly not a dozen. I have therefore decided that the midshipman from the *Liverpool* will remain where he is.

The Beothuk Expedition

Jonah Squibb

        I was more than a little chafed at Lieutenant Cartwright's refusal to have the ailing midshipman brought on board the shallop. To leave a fellow sailor to die in such a remote place, and at the hands of such a charlatan, would be unpardonable. All the same, I held my tongue, owing to the weather continuing wet and cold throughout the night. With nothing more than a lantern to heat the fore and aft cabins of the boat, it was just as well that the lad remained at the surgeon's house for the time being, especially as the surgeon was away and incapable of doing further harm.

        As for Lieutenant Cartwright, he had taken up residence in the merchant's premises, accompanied by his brother George, Reverend Stow and old Atkinson, the brother's cadaverous servant. They were to reside there as guests of Mr. Street while I remained on board with the crew. The arrangement served me well enough, as I wished to put our vessel into an improved state of order and comfort. I thought little of the fact that I had not actually been invited to stay at the house.

        The evening's work began with the makeshift canopy, which was taken down and rigged to better effect until it kept most of the rain off our heads. I then sent Bolger to find something fresh for our dinner and he returned with two enormous codfish and a quantity of their tongues. He knew of my fondness for tongues and, despite his disgust, he'd done me a great kindness in getting them. The fish we boiled on the boat's stove and the men ate it with biscuit and a plum duff, all the while eyeing me doubtfully as I floured and fried my cod tongues in lard. Only Greening would accept the offer of a few on his plate, saying that he was more partial to the cheeks himself.

Next I set about ordering the messes, assigning the forecastle to the seamen and claiming the aft cabin for the use of the warrant officers and myself. I had no doubt that Lieutenant Cartwright would change the arrangement when he returned from his comforts, though for now, the men were happy enough. To refer to the enclosed spaces fore and aft as cabins is perhaps to exaggerate their size. There was barely width or length for three men to sling their hammocks side-by-side, and just enough height to sit on low benches when the hammocks were stowed. Even when seated, the tallest amongst us, who happened to be me, had to be mindful of the beams. We managed to pass the night in reasonable, if chilly, comfort, the men serving in two watches under the warrant officers.

The next morning the weather continued poorly and I issued the first ration of rum early, so as to put a cheerful light on the day. I was not pleased, however, to observe petty officer Grimes gulping down his grog before demanding a share from his fellow *Liverpool*s. By then, I'd had some time to take the measure of these three, and I did not like what I saw. Grimes was a swaggering, thick-necked tar whom I'd already pegged for a tyrant. To quote Smollett, whom I'd been reading the day before: "He had all the outward signs of a sot; a sleepy eye, a rubicund face, and a carbuncled nose. He seemed to be a little out at the elbows, had marvelous foul linen, and his breeches were not very sound; but he assumed an air of importance." The other two sailors, a wizened Cornishman named Rundle and a near-idiot lad named Jenkins, were bullied by the petty officer at every turn. Jenkins, a slack-jawed and glassy-eyed youth, seemed to take the greater part of the abuse.

A short time after the incident with the grog, I saw Grimes

approach the boatswain and heard him ask for leave to go ashore. Had he known our Mr. Frost better, he would never have committed such folly. Or else he would have been suspicious of the pleasant manner in which the boatswain asked the reason for his request. Grimes, suspecting nothing, told him of a widow who sold rum in the parlour of her house and that he would stand the boatswain a tot if he joined him. It had not escaped my attention that our new crewmen were short on discipline, owing no doubt to having been left so long without supervision. Nor had this state of affairs gone unnoticed by the boatswain, who began putting things to right from that moment. I took my leave for the surgeon's house as he launched an oath-laden tirade against the hapless Grimes.

I had stationed Greening at the house in case of the surgeon's return and I found him awake and at his post when I arrived. He was cut from a different cloth than the others, with a plain, innocent face and an eagerness to please. He also possessed a shy and awkward manner that belied his physical strength and quickness of mind. I had high hopes of him, not only because he was a fellow Newfoundlander but also because he was at home in the rigging and had the makings of a fine topman. I sent the lad back to the shallop and seated myself by the midshipman's bed. To my surprise and delight, he was beginning to show signs of recovery. His skin was now dry to the touch and the woman said he'd been quiet through much of the night. She had ignored my earlier objections and had been administering a drink of boiled dandelion juice and spruce beer, with favourable results. I thanked her sincerely, which impressed her much less than the shilling, which disappeared into the folds of her shawl.

I was undecided whether it was God or Fate that had placed me in Bonavista to watch over this young man. It had to be more than mere coincidence, for I will tell you now that I loved him as a brother. He was as brave a sailor as ever stowed a hammock and as fine a friend as any man could wish. We had sailed together on the old *Northumberland* when he was a mere child and I his senior at the age of eighteen, which was now his present age. We were shipmates a few months only, but in that time the bond between us had been forged as strong as any steel, owing to what we had suffered and survived together.

The boy was none other than Friday Froggat, so named for the day of his birth, his mother having exhausted her store of names on his nineteen older siblings. He and I had maintained our friendship and correspondence over the years, but I'd heard nothing of him for the last six months or more. It was not an unusual length of time for a letter to catch up with a ship, though for all that, I was astonished to discover that the two of us had been serving in the same squadron without knowing it.

As for his health, Froggat was far from cured of his disease or the surgeon's treatments. However, I allowed myself to think that he stood half a chance with a friend at his side. Observing him for the first time in daylight, I saw that the exposed parts of his body were free of all but the faintest blemishes, excepting a half-dozen scars from cutlass and shot. A victim in whom the scurvy is well advanced would normally be covered in livid spots and open sores. His mouth hung open in sleep and I pulled back his lip, observing no sign of the inflamed gums and fetid breath that accompany the disease. His breathing was also regular and unlaboured, which gave me hope that the worst had passed.

At his very best Froggat was no balm for sore eyes and now he was a pitiful sight indeed. His front teeth, fashioned from polished whalebone, lay on the window ledge. Their absence gave him the appearance of a man much older than eighteen years. His body was emaciated and astonishingly ripe after two weeks of fevered sweating and his long red hair was a tangled mess. As a boy he'd been small for his age and in early manhood his stature remained that of an adolescent. His face had also retained some of the features of his youth, though an ever-present squint had prematurely deepened the lines around his eyes and the freckles on his pale face were darker and more numerous. But for all that, he looked better than he had the night before. The woman brought another cup of the hot, bitter drink and by early afternoon I thought that he'd improved half as much again. When I made ready to return to the shallop he was sleeping peacefully with a hint of colour to his cheek.

The rain and wind had diminished over the course of the morning, which was an unwelcome change. Any improvement in the weather would mean our departure from Bonavista before Froggat was restored to health and duty. I hastened to the boat and was greeted by the sight of Grimes and Rundle seated on the stagehead in the drizzle. Their clothes were wet through and they were plainly miserable, and in passing I noticed some discoloration around the eye of the petty officer. On board I was saluted by Bolger and Frost, who were mending a sail beneath the canopy. Greening and Jenkins were splicing a rope nearby. Excepting the two men in the rain, everything seemed in order and the crew well occupied. I was tempted to ask the obvious question but I kept my silence, as was often the wisest course in these matters, and judged that the ill discipline of our new sailors might now be a thing of the past.

"And how be the lad up yonder, sir?" Bolger asked as he laid his sewing aside.

"Improving by the hour, I'm pleased to say."

"Aye, and good news it is, sir," the gunner said. "I minds him from the old *Northumberland*, right enough. A proper young spark, he were." He took up his long-stemmed pipe and used the sail needle to stuff a piece of tobacco leaf into the bowl.

"The scurvy is it, Mister Squibb?" Frost asked. I nodded and he shook his head knowingly. "I were on the *Audacious* when it killed every second man and I were nearly one of 'em. All the old wounds I had come back on me like the day I fetched 'em. There was cuts from ten years afore that opened up and bled, fresh as could be. I even had a musket ball, what were given me by a French marine, work its way out o' me lower back."

The boatswain shook his grizzled head while the younger sailors listened closely. "A terrible affliction is what it is, sir. Many's the man been put over the side in less than a week. Yer Mister Froggat is a strong one to last this long."

"Aye, that he be," Bolger put in. "And he deserves a damned

sight more than to be left to die in this stink of fish." Here the gunner was beginning to tread soft ground. While he and Frost were accustomed to speaking plainly in my company, I wasn't about to make the ordinary seamen privy to such frank sentiments.

"That is not for us to decide, Mister Bolger," I said with a firmness that did not go unnoticed.

"Right ye are, sir," he mumbled. "I were only speaking in personal terms, like."

"Feel free to speak your mind when you are alone, Mister Bolger," I said. "Which is to say, never while you are on a boat."

My words were directed as much to the hands as they were to the gunner. I glanced at Greening and Jenkins as they pretended to concentrate on their work, and only then did the peculiar nature of Bolger's comment strike home. He could not have known what had passed between Lieutenant Cartwright and myself regarding the midshipman. Was he merely guessing or had something occurred in my absence?

"I must ask, Mister Bolger," I said, "why you should think that Mister Froggat would be left behind."

I could tell from the shift of his eyes that something had indeed happened while I was away. It was also plain, after my rebuke, that he was reluctant to speak of it openly.

"Perhaps we might have a hand of whist in the cabin," I said, "while Mister Frost summons those wretches out of the rain."

We ducked into the stern berth and sat facing each other in the cramped space. "Now then, what is this?" I demanded. "Has Lieutenant Cartwright been aboard?"

"Aye, sir," the gunner replied, running a hand over his speckled scalp.

"Well? Speak up, man. What did he want?"

"I aren't certain, sir, except he were plainly looking fer something. Poked his head into the cabins and gawked around the barrels, he did. Seemed a shade disappointed that he didn't find what he were seeking."

"And from that you believe that he was looking for Mister Froggat?"

"Aye, sir. From that and the orders he give to me and Hard Frost, sir."

"Orders? What orders were you given?"

The gunner eyed me uneasily. "Lieutenant Cartwright says we isn't to let anyone on board the boat, sir. Excepting the crew, of course." His tone was apologetic as he added, "No exceptions nor excuses, neither. He were most plain on that point, sir."

It was now evident that the first lieutenant did not trust me to obey his instructions. That he should regard me with suspicion was mildly insulting, although he was far from wrong to take that view. I had no plan to smuggle Froggat on board, but neither did I have any intention of leaving him behind.

Nehemiah Grimes

The devil take the lot o' them damned *Guernseys*, and specially that bastard Frost. Oh, ye needn't worry, I'll have back at 'em. Just mark my words. And when I does, it'll be Frost what gets it first, ye can be sure o' that. No man raises his hand to Nehemiah Grimes without getting it returned tenfold.

Justice and liberty, that's what I'll be having. Like what that feller John Wilkes been preaching in London. A man's got no goddamn rights nor priv'leges no more, he says, and don't us poor seamen know it! Our own cap'n leaves us here with a sickly middie and along comes another and takes us up like so many wharf rats. No justice and no liberty, just like Wilkes says.

More's the pity 'cause we had us as sweet a watch here as any man could ask. The run o' the town and no one barking at us or flicking them ropes. Only the three of us and as much rum as we could hold. Plus that lively widow woman when the fancy took. Just the thing for a man who's been a-sea these long months.

But it were too good to last, weren't it? Oh yes, too good by half. Along come this crowd o' popinjay officers and now it's yes sir, no sir and kiss me arse at noon, sir. And what about them fine gentlemen passengers, eh? They'll be eating what little grub there is and doing nothing to help sail this fish box, 'cept for treating us tars like scullions. Cartwright's brother, now there's a queer one with his guns and his servant and never putting his hand to a rope. And that whingy chaplain what starts praying when a bit o' spray comes over the bow.

Then we got that young Mr. Squibb from the *Guernsey*, with the unholy name o' Jonah. I never heard of such an ill-founded name for a sailor, but that's not the only strange thing about him. He's set on saving that sickly mid when it's plain the little bugger is three parts dead. And another thing. When he's not playing wet-nurse, he's sitting in the sternsheets with his nose in a book, which is something that no good never comes of, if ye asks me. No odds though, 'cause he's still a *Guernsey*, and they're all of a feather.

And then that fool Cartwright goes and nearly drowns the lot of us. If that weren't enough, now he says we're off to look for Red Indians! Goddamned fool is what he is and make no mistake. But the biggest fool of all is that Frost, if he thinks he can get the best of Nehemiah Grimes. He'll know he picked on the wrong one when he feels cold steel in his ribs some dark night. Just see if he don't. We'll soon find out how hard the Frost is, now won't we, my jolly lads? Oh yes, we will. Everyone who did old Grimsey wrong will get what he deserves. Wilkes and liberty, that's what I says. No justice, no king!

Jonah Squibb

On the next day I observed a further improvement in Froggat's condition. I arrived at the house to find him sitting up in bed and drinking a thin soup with the help of his caretaker. His mind was still clouded and he seemed not to know me at first until I called him by name and asked if he did not know his old friend. At that, his eyes gave the smallest flicker of recognition. It was all too brief and he fell once more into the dull exhaustion that would mark the rest of my visit. All the same, I was pleased to see the fever lessened and that he'd regained a state approaching consciousness.

I returned to the shallop at noon and imparted the news to the men, which was received with more approval by the *Guernsey*s than by his own shipmates. These *Liverpool*s were a surly lot, though much less bold in attitude since the boatswain's lesson in naval discipline. On this particular afternoon, I noted that Rundle and Jenkins were especially indolent and went about their duties as if they were half asleep. Fortunately for them, I was in a high good humour and ordered a ration of grog to celebrate the change in Froggat's health.

While our meal of salted pork lay in the steep tub, the men took their leisure with the half-pint of watered rum and a little tobacco for their pipes. I do not regret allowing them this indulgence but I do regret the sudden arrival of Lieutenant

Cartwright. I was laughing with the warrant officers at some joke or other when I heard him address me by name. I turned to see him standing upon the stage, his face a portrait of stern disapproval. I jumped to my feet, calling the crew to order as I lifted my hat. He acknowledged me with a stiff little bow and cast a critical eye over the vessel.

"I see you have things in hand, Mister Squibb," he said, his sarcasm evident as he eyed my cup. "Yet, I cannot but wonder at your ease when so much needs doing."

I was too astonished for an immediate reply and from the corner of my eye I saw Bolger's eyebrows arch in disbelief. Since coming into Bonavista, the men had repaired every sail, replaced and spliced every rope and even remounted the guns. This was to say nothing of the thorough cleansing with vinegar they'd given the vessel, or of the ordered state of her cargo and rigging.

The lieutenant pursed his lips and scrutinized the shallop in an effort to find something at fault. Seeing nothing, he took a different tack by announcing that we would require additional foodstuffs and that I should collect them immediately from Mister Street's store. I was again astounded at the man's arrogance, for how could he know that we were in need of anything when he'd spent so little time aboard?

"Another thing, Mister Squibb. In preparation for our voyage, you will be kind enough to organize our company according to rank. The officers and gentlemen will be berthed in the stern cabin and the warrant officers and servants in the forecastle. The hands will mess on the deck, as I think you have made it sufficiently comfortable for that purpose."

I saw the seamen exchange dark looks of resentment. "As you wish, sir," I replied.

"You may expect us aboard following dinner. We sail on the evening tide."

My mind was racing even as he made his way between the reeking barrels of cod liver oil and across the field to Mockbeggar House. How could we sail this evening when Froggat was barely able to sit upright? If I left him now that quacksalver surgeon would surely return and he would never recover. I grappled with the problem for a few minutes and merely succeeded in confounding myself. Alas, I am no mental wizard and have no genius for quick solutions. I would need time to think, though time was exactly what I lacked.

Meanwhile, there were provisions to get on board and a dozen other matters to attend to before the tide turned. I quickly organized the men, leaving most of them to tasks on board while Jenkins and Greening accompanied me to the plantation storeroom. We were already well provisioned but to please the lieutenant I ordered small quantities of dried beans, salted cod and pickled cabbage. As the clerk weighed and measured, I paced the store and considered the problem of Friday Froggat.

The afternoon passed and our party of gentlemen came on board, their bellies filled with the merchant's food and fine wine. The evening was fair with a moderate southwesterly breeze and after we'd slipped our ropes I took us out of the harbour under reefed main and jib. Lieutenant Cartwright had disappeared into the aft cabin and so I laid a course north-northwest for Cape Freels. Compared to our first outing, it was a different boat that heeled to the wind that evening. The sails were a patchwork of repairs, it was true, but they were as sturdy as any newly issued by the naval dockyard. The stores in the waist had been re-stowed to best advantage and we were making five or six knots on the long southerly swell.

It had not gone unnoticed by the crew that our guests, the Reverend Stow and George Cartwright, had employed their time ashore in augmenting their meagre wardrobe. The latter was dressed as a common fisherman and took no small delight in his "masquerade," as he called it. His costume consisted of a pair of canvas breeches and a coarse woolen tunic, topped by an oiled canvas cloak. He also had a hat of the kind that fishermen wear to keep the spray from going down their necks. As for the chaplain, he was arrayed in a black frock coat that was shiny from use, a cast-off periwig and knee-length breeches with old-fashioned buckles. Frost and I stood on the little stern deck, he at the tiller and I at the con, while our clerical passenger promenaded amidships. The boatswain shook his head at the sight and muttered: "*Bobby Shaftoe went to sea, silver buckles on his knee. He'll come back and marry me, pretty Bobby Shaftoe!*"

We were a good half-hour upon our course when the first lieutenant emerged from the stern cabin. He stood in the waist below us with his hands clasped behind his back, assuming the air of a captain upon his quarterdeck. Had we been possessed of a quarterdeck, he might have been more convincing. I watched him examine the angle of the spars and the set of the sails, and then heard him order an adjustment to the trim of the staysail. The object in question was, in my own opinion, perfectly aligned to capitalize on the wind. But for reasons that I was only beginning to understand, he wished to have it changed straight away. The order was carried out and the effect was immediate, with the loss of a good half-knot of speed. I heard the boatswain groan as Cartwright looked up at me, challenging any criticism. I betrayed no emotion and kept my eyes upon the compass until he returned to the cabin. Then, at my nod, the sail was returned to its original setting.

The night slipped away without incident and by dawn we were past Cape Freels and the Cabot Isles and had changed our course northwest to the Wadhams. Bolger had the middle watch and I relieved him a few hours after midnight to take my lunar observations. An hour later, I steered us between the bare white rocks of Offer Wadham and Small Island as dawn spread its glow in the east. Our passage between the islands caused flocks of noddies and tinkers to rise screeching from their nests. A multitude of Great Auks splashed around our hull and dove as we sailed amongst them. These flightless birds, which the fishermen call penguins, were said to exist in infinite numbers along this coast. Funk Island was named for the smell that marked the greatest concentration of them.

The noise of the birds brought all hands out of the hammocks and about their morning business. Since we were not on board a man-of-war, the routine was relaxed, without the pipes and orders that regulate every minute of life on such a vessel. Old Atkinson, Mr. Cartwright's worn and silent servant, found a sack of oats and busied himself with making a pot of burgoo for our breakfast. His master grumbled about his guns not being loaded and the loss of a sporting shoot, but the old man paid him no heed.

The rest of the crew occupied themselves with plaiting their long pigtails or relieving themselves over the side. On such a small and crowded vessel there was no privacy, which affected none at all but the Reverend Stow. I watched him take a bucket and modestly seat himself upon it behind a row of barrels. This caused much amusement among the tars and their laughter roused Lieutenant Cartwright. He came out from the cabin, looked sternly about and let fly his water over the gunwale.

His business completed, he joined me on the poop as I placed the shallop on a heading that would bring us between Fogo Island and the Little Fogos. We exchanged a few words about our course and situation and he nodded his approval, even allowing himself a smile when I told him that we would enter Fogo Harbour well before noon. I asked him whether he expected to find Mr. Palliser and the *Guernsey* there, to which he replied, "I should think not, unless the governor has already seized the *Valeur*. He is determined to put an end to this French business and he will search every cove in the Bay of Notre Dame to meet that end."

"And what of the *Liverpool*?" I asked. "If she is at Fogo, will her captain expect his people returned?"

He shrugged and grabbed a halyard to steady himself. "Mister Palliser has said that the *Liverpool*s are to remain under my command until we have completed our task. I see no reason why that may change."

What I'd hoped to hear was that the three sailors would be returned to their frigate, for in spite of some improvement I could not bring myself to trust them. Something might be made of the boy Jenkins, I thought, but Grimes and Rundle were accomplished idlers.

"I believe it is high time that I put a name to our worthy

little vessel," the lieutenant was saying. "In view of the importance of our mission, I think it hardly fitting that we continue to call her a common shallop." He sniffed the brisk morning air and rocked himself on his heels. "I have given the matter some consideration, Mister Squibb. Because she is as much a sloop as a shallop, henceforth we shall call her a sloop. It imparts a greater measure of dignity, does it not? And I believe that I shall name her HMS *Dove*, in honour of the task that has been laid before us."

He turned to me with a self-satisfied smile, even as I was thinking that it would take more than a lieutenant's fancy to turn a fishing boat into a naval sloop. And a sloop-of-war named the *Dove*? Before I could think of a suitable reply, we were startled by a sudden cry from the chaplain, and a very loud cry at that. In fact, it may have been a screech. We looked to see him stumbling from behind a hogshead with his breeches about his ankles.

"What the devil—" Mr. Cartwright exclaimed, even as the Reverend Stow snatched the wig from his head to cover his manhood. The sight of him would have struck me as the height of comedy, were it not for the words he managed to stammer.

"That b-barrel! Just there! The Lord protect us—there's s-something moving in it!"

John Cartwright

        Am I to be frustrated at every turn by weather and circumstance? Or else by human failing and deceit? The first of these I can do nothing about and the other is a trial borne by all who command. But this disregard for my orders is beyond the tolerance of any man. Were I a flogging officer, I would have one or two of my crew stretched across a gun at this very moment. They may thank their stars that I will not debase my principles to assert my authority.

        This morning our poor chaplain was near frightened out of his wits by a noise from one of the casks on deck. I ordered it opened and discovered the midshipman of the *Liverpool* hidden there. This is in clear violation of my order that only our own people be permitted on board. I confronted the man, who is plainly very ill, and demanded to know who had brought him to the *Dove*. He was scarcely sensible but was able to lie well enough, saying he had stowed himself away in hopes of rejoining his ship. I did not believe him for a moment, given his state of extreme weakness. But I am now in the maddening position of either denouncing him for a liar or accepting what he says. Of course, I cannot accuse him of untruths when I have no evidence to the contrary. All the same, I suspect our Mr. Squibb of having had a hand in it, and likely the warrant officers as well.

To add to my frustration, I find that I cannot rid myself of this unwanted stowaway. On our approach to Joe Batt's Arm we espied three topsails on the horizon, bearing east off Shoal Bay. These were surely the sails of our frigates *Tweed*, *Lark* and *Liverpool*, whose bows we would have crossed had we arrived an hour sooner. I was further impeded in ridding myself of the sickly boy when, on entering the arm, we discovered an outbreak of spotted fever amongst the inhabitants. I would have put him ashore except I had no desire to expose my crew to the affliction.

That the place should be infected is no surprise to me. The harbour is a cesspool of waste from the fishery and the brigs that are anchored there. Even the rats line the gunwales in hopes of deserting for something better. No doubt in winter the place returns to its natural state, when the harbour is abandoned and the tide and weather cleanse the land and water. But for now I kept our distance and hailed the boats for news of John Cousens.

The replies that were thrown back at me were a shock to my ears. I may only imagine their effect upon the sensibilities of one so delicate as Reverend Stow. These are plainly the drunkest, roughest collection of blasphemers this side of Christendom, and their captains are no better. One of them even threw a bottle at my head when I addressed him, and but for the pitch of our vessels it might have caused me a grievous injury. Mr. Bolger offered to put a ball across the deck of this festering scow, and while the prospect was attractive, I would have none of it. For now the spotted fever prevents my ordering an immediate arrest, but the lout will know my justice at another time.

The only information I have been able to obtain is that Cousens is at either Toulinguet or Fogo Harbour. I have ordered Lieutenant Squibb to set a course for the latter place at once. I am grateful for an excuse to quit this foul inlet, which to my mind is typical of the entire northern district. It has become a wild and lawless place since the last war, with nothing of the order and religion that should mark an outpost of England.

Derek Yetman

Of course, this state of affairs suits many of the merchants who operate here, for it allows them to do as they wish without regard for the law. I fear that this stew of anarchy breeds notions against the Red Indians as well. Those involved in trade will naturally seek to protect their interests, while their ignorant servants believe they must kill the savages or be killed themselves. Captain Palliser has put his faith in my ability to strike a truce. I have no doubt that I shall prevail, for truth and justice are always on the side of the righteous. I am therefore determined to capture an emissary of these people, to whom we may demonstrate our good intentions. And find one we shall, so that they may know the compassion of our Sovereign King.

Jonah Squibb

    Joe Batt's Arm had little to recommend it, aside from its proximity to the fishing grounds. Named by Captain Cook for a relative of his wife, it was a narrow inlet with a great many rocks that soon impeded our progress. With Lieutenant Cartwright's attention elsewhere, I had the canvas taken in and the men put to the sweeps. We rowed up the harbour and came alongside a number of brigs, where the lieutenant called for news of John Cousens. The reception he received was far from civil and some of the captains declared they had the spotted fever on board. I suspect that they took us for a press gang and were in no great hurry to join, or to rejoin, His Majesty's Navy.

    Relying upon what little we could learn, we departed the arm at eight bells and struck out for Fogo Harbour. Lieutenant Cartwright was most anxious that we arrive there as soon as we could, perhaps out of concern for the health of Reverend Stow. The stench of fish offal and human waste in the arm had been bad enough but the southwesterly wind had become baffled and confused among the headlands. The result was a choppy sea that caused the chaplain to lose what little colour he had, to say nothing of the contents of his stomach.

    We were crossing the mouth of Shoal Bay when I gave the helm to the boatswain and went forward to check on Froggat.

He was lodged in a hammock beneath the canopy and next to him was a sling containing Reverend Stow. The chaplain groaned at every movement of the vessel and acted as if he might expire at any moment. I ignored him and looked to my friend, whose face was grey and cold to the touch. This was not a symptom of scurvy that I had encountered before and my concern grew as I discovered his pulse to be very weak.

The chaplain was not to be outdone for attracting sympathy. He groaned most horribly and fixed his mournful eyes upon me. "Mister Squibb," he whispered hoarsely, "I fear I am done for, sir. Done for, I say."

It took every whit of patience I could muster to reply, "Nay, sir. You will recover soon enough, I am certain."

"Ah, but sir," he moaned, "You have no conception. Can you not sail this boat in a more delicate fashion? I declare that any man who would go to sea for pleasure would go to hell for a pastime."

My impatience was tempered by surprise on hearing Samuel Johnson quoted from so unexpected a quarter. I parried with a quote of my own, saying, "Your opinion of my sailing skills has been noted, sir. But I must tell you that criticism is a study by which men grow important at small expense."

The vicar opened a watery eye. "My apologies, young man," he said. "I believe I may have misjudged you."

I filled a ladle with water from the scuttlebutt and held it for him to drink. "On that point, I believe your judgment to be sound, sir," I replied.

He looked at me sharply and slurped the water. Lying back in the hammock, he sighed, closed his eyes and asked, "Are you sincere in your opinion that I shall not die?"

"You have been seasick before," I said. "A man used to vicissitudes cannot be so easily dejected."

The eye opened slightly. "Johnson again?"

"I see that you suffer no mental impairment, Reverend. I think we may safely pronounce you out of danger. We will soon be in an open reach and the turbulence will subside."

The Beothuk Expedition

"Your friend, Mister Squibb—will he live?"

I looked at Froggat's ashen face and replied, "I can only pray that he does. There is nothing more I can do for him."

The watch was nearly ended when I threw the tiller over and changed our tack to beat close-hauled into the harbour of Fogo. The islands that crowd the entrance make it an interesting business but with smart work, we came within the shelter of the surrounding hills and struck our sails. The chaplain had by then recovered and was the first one into the jolly boat when Greening let go the bower.

A short time later the crowded boat ran onto the beach and to no one's surprise, our passengers and first lieutenant made straight for the largest house. Lieutenant Cartwright paused long enough to say that I was to be ready to sail at a moment's notice. He also handed me a small packet of papers and instructed me to read them at my earliest convenience. I thrust these into my pocket and promptly forgot about them, being more concerned with matters related to the boat and crew.

The evening crept upon us as the men loosened the sails to dry and the boatswain fired the stove for our supper. The little cove was quiet except for the last of the day's splitting and salting, and here and there small groups of people walked the path around the harbour. Sheep and goats grazed on the steep hillsides, and high above them the gulls wheeled in the failing light. It seemed a pleasant enough place, and from across the water came the cheerful notes of a fiddle. While we waited for our meal, I measured out the evening grog, taking care to observe the behaviour of the *Liverpool*s. I noticed that Greening did not sit with them, but kept to himself while they gathered on the forecastle.

I had by now confirmed my suspicion that Grimes held sway over the others. He finished his rum in a few quick gulps and held the empty mug to Jenkins and Rundle, who paid their fealty without complaint. Strictly speaking, no man was permitted more than his fair share, although the practice of trading spirits was a long-standing part of the shipboard economy. In this instance, however, I could not believe that it

Derek Yetman

was done for any reason but fear. I had no doubt that Grimes kept his status as ringleader through the threat of violence, if not the act itself.

After our meal of salted pork and cabbage, I retired to the stern cabin, which had reverted to Bolger, Frost and myself in the absence of the lieutenant. There I remembered the papers he'd given me and I began to read them by the light of a lantern. Truth to tell, I was not far advanced when I found myself succumbing to the drink and the meal, and before long I was entombed in a deep and dreamless slumber. I cannot say how long I slept but it was completely dark when an unearthly shriek impaled the night and brought me wide awake. My feet hit the boards in an instant and I groped for the door. I emerged onto the moonlit deck, grabbing a cutlass from the rack as I went.

I could not say what I expected, whether a terrible accident or a desperate affray. And yet, nothing seemed to be amiss. Bolger and Greening were standing in the waist, looking at something that lay at their feet. At that moment the object of their puzzled attention screamed again. In three strides I was with them and saw poor Froggat thrashing about on his back, his eyes wide with terror. I knelt by his side, restraining him and calling for water. In soothing tones I calmed him enough for Greening and me to lift him into his hammock. For a moment he appeared on the verge of speaking, but then his eyes fell abruptly shut and he slipped again into a state of insensibility.

This alarmed me very much and the more so because there was nothing I could do for him. I was now convinced that his strange illness was not related to scurvy, for his body had recovered entirely from that disease. What caused him such anguish might have been mental or nervous in nature, but all I could do was hope that this latest trial would pass. I turned to the others, who were watching with the air of a funeral party. "I will take the watch, Mister Bolger," I said. "Hail the others and send them aft."

"Aye, aye, sir. You there, Greening. Send the *Liverpool*s along and turn in yerself. Look lively now."

The young sailor went forward and I stood with the two

warrant officers, looking down at Froggat.

"Can ye say what it is, sir?" Bolger asked.

I shook my head. "I cannot. Have either of you ever seen these symptoms?" Before they could answer, we were interrupted by the sudden return of Greening, who appeared anxious to tell us something.

"Well?" Frost demanded. "What is it, then?"

"They isn't there, Mister Frost."

"What do you mean, not there?" the boatswain fairly shouted. "Who's not there?"

Greening swallowed hard and plucked up his courage. "Grimes and Rundle, Mister Frost. Their hammocks is empty, though Jenkins is there and fast asleep."

Frost let out a roar that could have roused the very fish on the flakes. "By God, I'll have their gizzards!" His face had turned a fiery red. "They must've swam ashore. Permission to go and find the blackguards, Mister Squibb."

"Go," I said. "And go with him, Mister Bolger. Find them before Cartwright does or we'll have the devil to pay." I was tempted to go as well until I remembered my orders. The thought of the lieutenant returning to find three parts of his crew absconded was not a pleasant one. As the warrant officers rowed into the darkness that lay around us I turned to Greening. "Bring Jenkins to me."

The boy wore a defiant look when he was brought aft. He was tousled and without a shirt, having been roughly hauled from his hammock. "Where have they gone?" I demanded. He refused to answer at first but his brazen exterior soon dissolved under my glare. That simple mind was in anguish, I could tell, as he weighed his chances between Grimes and myself. He did not possess the ability to be artful and after a moment he mumbled something about not having heard them leave the forecastle.

This very nearly caused me to lose my temper, as I do not take kindly to being played the fool. It was clearly something that he'd been coached to say, for the crew slept head-to-toe in the forecastle and a man could not fart without waking the

Derek Yetman

others. "Perhaps your hearing will improve when the boatswain returns," I said ominously.

Although I detest gratuitous punishment, I am not averse to the threat of it to get at the truth. This is not always effective, of course, as many men become hardened to the lash and make no more of a flogging than of pricking a finger. Among the younger hands, however, there is often a great reluctance to meet with the cat. Having witnessed or even heard of such punishments, they are left with the greatest horror of it. In this instance my threat worked admirably and young Jenkins sang like a canary.

In a voice that was thin with fear, he told me that the others had swum ashore late in the first watch when Bolger and Greening were checking the bilge. Grimes had gone in search of drink, he said, and had taken Rundle with him. They planned to return before the next watch, in hopes that no one would be the wiser. I was not surprised to hear this, considering what I'd observed of Grimes. That he and Rundle might be attempting to desert had also entered my mind, though it would be a fool's bid on such an isolated island. The greater puzzle to me was that the petty officer possessed ready money to purchase spirits, just as he had at Bonavista. It was a rare thing for a seaman to have coins in his pocket while at sea. His basic needs were met and the greater portion of his pay was withheld until the voyage ended and the ship paid off.

I said nothing of this but as punishment for his complicity, I ordered Jenkins to stand watch for the remainder of the night. It was a lenient sentence and I believe it surprised him, for how could he know that my motive was to win him to my side? I reasoned that in the days and weeks to come I would need every thread of loyalty that I could cultivate. The truth is that I was beginning to have the gravest doubts about the future of this expedition. Mr. Cartwright had yet to inspire me with confidence and many in our party seemed unfit for what lay ahead.

Shortly before dawn, while I was preparing my excuses for the first lieutenant, Bolger and Frost appeared alongside with the two culprits. Grimes was plainly under the influence of drink and had consumed enough to acquire a belligerent courage. He cursed and threatened Frost for his rough handling, though I saw no evidence of cuts or bruises upon him. I had expected to see them in worse condition and I threw the gunner a questioning glance.

"We thought it best not to mark 'em, sir," he said, "lest Mister Cartwright know what was up, like. We reckoned ye'd want to deal with 'em yourself." I nodded my approval, when in fact I was at a complete loss as to what I should do. I could order a punishment, except it would have to be severe enough to match the offence and that would be impossible to hide from the first lieutenant. Or perhaps a more subtle approach was called for. Grimes and Rundle had formed a tight little knot that was in need of splitting if we were ever to have peace on this vessel. And perhaps I had just the means of bringing it about.

The two men sat on the deck where they'd fallen, the petty officer drunkenly brazen while the others awaited my judgment. "Mister Bolger," I said, "prepare this man for punishment."

The gunner dragged the snarling Grimes to his feet. "Wilkes and liberty!" he slurred as Bolger stripped him of his shirt. "No justice, no King!"

So that was it. Recent events in England had already begun to infect the fleet. John Wilkes was the editor of *The North Briton* and his radical ideas of freedom and justice had inflamed the lower classes over the preceding months. He had offended many powerful men and had even been wounded in a duel with the secretary of the treasury. Once a colonel of militia and a member of parliament, he had been charged with sedition, libel and obscenity after attacking the authority of the King and the House of Commons.

I was certainly aware of the man's influence upon the idle and dissolute of England, but I was surprised to hear a sailor espouse his cause. London's poor had rioted at Wilkes' trial in April and had shown more interest in looting than in the principles of social justice. They had tried to free him from King's Bench Prison and when the army was ordered up a number of the mob had been shot dead in St. George's Fields. This had led to more violence, with the rioters attacking the houses of the Lord Mayor and the Prime Minister himself. As for Wilkes, he'd been sentenced in June to two years' imprisonment and that was the last I'd heard of him. Until now.

All of this went through my mind in an instant as Grimes was being seized to the barrel of the nearest swivel gun. With his shirt removed, it was clear that he was no stranger to the lash. The scars on his back told as much of his past as any court martial record. Greening could not hide his pleasure at tying the man's arms, his grin provoking Grimes to swear even louder. When the task was done, the crew stood back and waited. I cleared my throat and adopted what I hoped was a grave and official voice:

"Nehemiah Grimes of His Majesty's Ship *Liverpool*—" The men were silent, their faces expectant. "You are to be punished for willfully disobeying the lawful orders of the commander of this vessel. My judgment is that your ration of spirits will be stopped from this moment on. You will also take a dozen lashes in the bargain." The warrant officers exchanged looks of dismay. So light a sentence was unheard of. "Bring the cat, Mister Frost," I said.

"Aye, sir." The instrument of discipline was brought out, its tarred grip tapering to nine strands of yard-long, tightly plaited leather. The boatswain flexed his arm in preparation, but I raised a hand to stop him.

"Seaman Rundle. On your feet." Assisted by Bolger's grip on his ear, the man rose quickly. He was small and dark and one eye was clouded with cataracts. The good eye looked at me with half-hearted defiance. "Hand him the cat, Mister Frost," I said. "Rundle will administer the dozen." The astonished man's mouth moved wordlessly as the boatswain thrust the whip into his hand and spun him around.

"Now then," I said. "For every lash that Mister Frost deems too lenient, you will earn an additional two for yourself. Do I make myself understood?" He nodded weakly as Grimes renewed his torrent of threats and abuse, this time directed at his shipmate. Rundle laid the first stroke across his back and Grimes roared, more in outrage than pain. The boatswain judged it to be the stroke of a kitten and added two to Rundle's own punishment. He did not make the same mistake twice and this time Grimes had reason to howl. He continued to howl until the dozen were given and then the petty officer savagely administered the twelve and two that were Rundle's reward.

The immediate result of this was just as I'd hoped. The two offenders were in a rage at each other, in equal parts because of the pain and the humiliation. The warrant officers were impressed and Greening was delighted. I was somewhat pleased myself, having driven a wedge not only between Grimes and Rundle but between them and young Jenkins. I had also punished them effectively without the excessive force that would have disabled them from working. In short, I was wonderfully proud of myself, having sat in judgment with all the wisdom of Solomon. Or so I thought. In hindsight, I am able to see clearly the vanity of my assumptions. But is that not the province of every young man? As a junior officer I had much to learn about my own nature, to say nothing of the nature of those whom I had the misfortune to command.

George Cartwright

        I declare that I am most impressed with these enterprising countrymen of mine. At Bonavista and here at Fogo I have encountered a good many fellows who seem to be making tidy fortunes for themselves. I only agreed to accompany my brother on this voyage for the excellent shooting to be had, but now my mind has turned firmly to the subject of trade. I have observed that the area is exceedingly rich in salmon and furs, and only a handful of traders are exploiting these opportunities. In fact, there are surprisingly few individuals involved in this harvest, apart from a few local planters and the agents of wealthy men in Poole.

        The cod fishery, on the other hand, is quite profitable but overly crowded. My brother tells me the French have some 450 vessels and 15,000 men on their shore, while we have nearly 20,000 men of our own. The two fleets are expected to take a million quintals this year, which is more than one hundred million pounds of salted fish! By contrast, only a half-million pounds of dried salmon are produced, even though it fetches a handsome price on the European market. The same may be said of the fur harvest, the numbers being quite small compared to what exists for the taking.

        I have been casting my eye about for a promising venture since leaving Minorca. The army was all well and good during the war, with hardly a dull moment, but in peace it holds few attractions for a man of my parts. Great events are taking place throughout the empire and the time was never better for a man to make his mark. I have heard that Samuel Hearne, the former Navy chap, is about to begin a two-year trek from Hudson's Bay to the Arctic Ocean in search of the Northwest Passage. A Scot named James Finlay has reached the Saskatchewan River far to the west of Canada and has established his own trading post. And of course my brother has been cracking on about this fellow Cook. Great adventures are afoot and here in Newfoundland there is room for a man to test his mettle. Or perhaps in Labrador, where trade is still in its infancy.

The biggest drawback would appear to be our poor relations with the Indians and Esquimaux. I am told that in Labrador they are most intractable and we have had only limited success in convincing them to barter. Brother John informs me that just this summer past they were bold enough to plunder a fishing station near Fort York. Of course, Lieutenant Lucas of the garrison there quickly taught them a lesson, killing twenty of the thieves and capturing several others. Captain Palliser also had the foresight to send three of the prisoners to England. They will soon learn that the great tribe of Englishmen is too numerous and powerful to oppose, and that they would do well to trade with us in peace.

It seems that on the island we have even less to show after nearly two centuries of coming here. Captain Palliser is of the opinion that trade with the natives will never progress unless we establish a peaceful coexistence with them, and I am inclined to agree. I have learned a good deal about these savages since coming to Fogo. The people here often encounter them in the neighbouring islands. They call them Red Indians because they daub their bodies and clothing with red ochre clay—most curious, to be sure. One man has seen them travelling by canoe in search of eggs and shellfish and he says they are elusive creatures. I have a romantic notion of them silently paddling their boats of birch bark like wraiths in the mist of an evening. It is a singular, almost incredible fact, told to me by several people, that they journey as far out to sea as Funk Island, which is fully forty miles from the coast. They have been observed expertly spearing fish in the rivers, and in archery they are said to have an unerring hand. I am convinced that, with such skills and knowledge of the country, the Red Indians would make ideal partners in trade.

In reflecting upon this, I have struck upon a scheme that would advance such a goal. I envision the establishment of a royal reserve, a place that would give the Indians the protection they require, while allowing them access to the land. They would then be able to supply their own needs as well as our demand for furs. This seems to me a capital solution and one that I intend to propose to Governor Palliser at the earliest opportunity. And if I were to become the agent or custodian of this royal reserve, then so much the better! My fortune would be made, to say nothing of the excellent hunting to be had.

The Beothuk Expedition

Jonah Squibb

The morning after our arrival at Fogo I received a visit from Reverend Stow. He surprised me, in fact, by leaving the comfort of the agent's house and seeking me out on board the *Dove*. I was equally amazed to see that he was not wearing his wig. I do not wish to sound cruel but the stubble of his scalp reminded me very much of the prickly hide of an animal. The fancy was apparently shared by Frost, who crowed a verse as the chaplain approached in a hired skiff: "*As I went to Bonner, I met a pig without a wig, upon my word of honour!*"

To what we owed this particular honour was unclear until he came alongside and announced that he would value my company on a ramble over the nearby hills. I had no objection, having come to friendly terms with the chaplain through our common interest in Dr. Johnson's wit, but I explained that Lieutenant Cartwright's orders prevented me from going so far. He suggested instead that we stroll the path around the harbour, to which I agreed.

The harbour at Fogo was little different from hundreds of others along the coast, except there was a higher proportion of families than single fishing servants. Flakes dominated the shoreline, with scattered stages and tilts, and as we made our way among them the smells of salted fish and wood smoke permeated all. Men and women worked side-by-side, the men cleaning and splitting the morning's catch while the women attended to the salting and drying. Children cut the livers, carried water or salt and otherwise helped where they were needed. All worked steadily and without pause, for their labour in these three or four months of fair weather would have to carry them through the winter, whether they remained here or returned to their villages in England or Ireland.

I had that morning finished reading the papers that the lieutenant had given me. These consisted of an account of the Red Indians written by Mr. Joseph Banks, the noted naturalist. Banks had been to Newfoundland with Captain Palliser two years earlier and had given him a copy of his notes on the subject. This had been given to Lieutenant Cartwright and thence to me, so that we might learn more about the subjects of our mission.

It was the opinion of that eminent scientist, who was at that moment accompanying Mr. Cook on his expedition to the Pacific, that there were not more than five hundred Red Indians remaining on the island. Banks believed them to be principally situated on this very coast and inland of the Bay of Exploits. He wrote that the settlers live in a state of continual warfare with them, destroying their canoes, food and houses at every opportunity. This has been the practice for at least fifty years, so that the Indians look upon us in exactly the same light as we do them. They kill our people and steal traps and nets whenever they have the advantage.

There had been terrible atrocities on both sides and more in recent years, as salmoniers and furriers moved northward and inland. A few years earlier, a shipmaster named Scott and five others had been killed in the Bay of Exploits. The body of one of them was brought to St. John's with the arrows still in it. Even more recently, a Captain Hall, for whom Hall's Bay is named, was murdered on his plantation. Banks wrote of the manner in which the Indians scalp their victims, for they are not content with just the hair. They skin the entire face down to the mouth. He had seen such a scalp that was taken from a fisherman named Sam Frye. The Indians had possession of it for a full year, and when it was recovered the features were so well preserved that it was recognized immediately as belonging to the unfortunate Frye. Although Mr. Banks had heard many such stories about the cruelty of the Red Indians, he concluded that "if half of what I have written about them is true, it is more than I expect."

For their part, the settlers were no less savage, it seemed. The tales were sickening, and while Banks had difficulty believing them, there was every likelihood that they were founded upon an element of truth. It was in this frame of mind that I took the air with Reverend Stow. Given our purpose for being here, it was no surprise, therefore, when he opened our conversation on the very subject of the Red Indians. He spoke at some length about them and it soon became clear that he was less concerned with their persecution than with their spiritual salvation. It was also plain that he hadn't sought me out for my company alone, but rather to enlist me as an ally to his cause.

"I say, Mister Squibb," he brayed as we picked our way over the muddy track, "have I not seen you in attendance at my Sunday service on board the *Guernsey*?"

"You have, sir," I replied. "My guardian was a man of the cloth and I have no desire to break the church-going habit." I neglected to say that the habit was less than regular and that I was not without my share of vices.

The chaplain gave me a horsey grin and said, "Well spoken, young sir. There are many officers who are less attentive to their religious duties, as you are no doubt aware. Cards, whores and drink seem to be the new Trinity."

I thought for a moment that he was referring to the town as well as the divinity, but the wit was unintentional. I was nonetheless impressed by his frankness and replied that the Navy had always harboured its share of rakes and rascals.

"So it has, Mister Squibb," he said, "and, while it is not the policy of the Church to admit it, for many there is little hope of redemption. However—" he paused and blew his nose into an embroidered handkerchief, "—there is much that may be done for this poor tribe of Red Indians. They live in a state of ignorance and merely await the word of God to change their heathen ways."

"And what would you have them change?" I asked.

He shot me a look that bordered on suspicion. "Why, their warlike ways for one, sir."

"But what of our own people? They appear equally brutish. It makes one wonder whether we live in a state of war by nature."

He looked at me again, this time with the expression of one too clever to be tricked so easily. "Ah, but sir, you are using the argument of the philosopher Hobbes, with whom I cannot agree."

"Would you not agree," I countered, "that there are three natural causes of conflict amongst humans, as Hobbes suggests?"

"I would, sir. And as I recall they are competition, distrust and glory."

"Indeed. And here we have the first two in large measure and a goodly element of the third. I suggest that until we remove them we shall have no lasting peace with these people."

"You make an interesting point, Mister Squibb. But you will recall that these causes of war apply to man in his natural state, without the word of God to guide him."

"And how," I replied, "do you propose to convert the Red Indian when our own people set so poor an example of Christian virtue?" We stood to one side of the track to allow a dog-cart to pass. The large animal's tongue lolled in the morning heat and fish scales glittered in its matted black fur.

"This is a labour of faith, Mister Squibb," the chaplain said through his handkerchief. "Not of example. Proverbs tells us that the desire of the righteous shall be granted."

He was plainly avoiding my question but I chose not to press the point. He may not have the answer, I thought, but at least he has the conviction that the Indians' lives might be improved. He pocketed the handkerchief and looked at me, his eyes animated by a peculiar brightness.

The Beothuk Expedition

"Every human has the capacity for love, sir. Would you not agree?"

I thought of creatures like Grimes but acknowledged his point with a nod.

"It is this love that serves as the medium of conjunction between man and his Creator. Salvation for us all, you see, can only be brought about by our love for each other. It is this very love that will allow us to form a new heaven from the human race."

I could not say that I agreed with this, though he'd caught my interest with the sudden intensity of his manner and the fluttering and waving of his bony fingers.

"Of course, the new heaven could not be created before the Last Judgment," he said, "as described in the Revelation of St. John the Divine."

No doubt my blank look prompted him to quote: "I saw a new heaven and a new earth, for the first heaven and the first earth were passed away, and there was no more sea. And I saw the holy city, the new Jerusalem, coming from God out of heaven." He rolled his eyes ecstatically and added, "Now that the judgment has taken place, we are preparing for the great event. Imagine, sir, a new Jerusalem for mankind!"

He paused long enough for me to nod in feigned understanding. I was beginning to suspect that our odd, gangly chaplain was as mad as a hatter. "And when did this—this judgment—actually occur?" I asked.

The chaplain smiled happily. "Why, in 1757 of course."

I nodded again, not knowing what else to do.

"You see," he continued, "the new heaven will of course be populated by the souls of the devout, and also by the souls of those who existed in a natural state at the time of their passing. This includes individuals, even entire populations, who had no clear understanding of the Lord ... who knew little or nothing of Christianity, but who lived as God had created them."

I began to see a hint of light. "And this would apply to the souls of the Red Indians?" I offered.

"Precisely!" the chaplain beamed.

Derek Yetman

Lines from a poem of Alexander Pope came to my mind: *Lo, the poor Indian! Whose untutored mind sees God in clouds, or hears him in the wind.* It occurred to me that under Reverend Stow's plan of populating the new heaven, the owners of these coveted souls would first of all have to be dead.

"Have you read *The Journal of Dreams*, Mister Squibb?" he asked.

"I have not," I confessed. "Who is the author?"

Reverend Stow shook his stubbled head and clucked in mild rebuke. "My dear sir! Why, Emanuel Swedenborg, of course."

"Ah, yes," I said, feeling confidence return, "the mathematical philosopher and inventor."

My companion nodded so vigorously I feared he would do himself an injury. "Yes, yes!" he squealed, "and visionary theologian as well."

I searched the meager store of my memory for something more about Swedenborg. I knew that he was one of a multitude of intellectuals and lunatics who were seeking a reliable means of determining longitude at sea. His method required exact lunar tables, which depended upon the accuracy of John Harrison's marine chronometer. Of course, Harrison's invention had yet to be accepted by the Board of Longitude, which meant that Swedenborg's tables were questionable as well. Swedenborg, I recalled, was also said to commune with angels and had written treatises on his dreams of heaven and hell.

My mind drifted back to this marine chronometer, which was a subject of much discussion in the Navy. While we continued with our method of dead reckoning, which was little more than estimation, Harrison had brought his time-measuring instrument through four designs and many trials at sea. Each of these had been more successful than the last and the most recent test was to take place on Mr. Cook's expedition. But in spite of his success, Harrison was still considered "a mere mechanic" by Nevil Maskelyne, the Astronomer Royal.

We came to a fork in the path and I suggested that we retrace our steps. As we did so, the chaplain expanded upon his mission to populate this new heaven with the souls of heathen Indians. He went on at length and I soon found his logic too convoluted to follow. When we came to where Greening was waiting with the jolly boat, I bade him good day with some relief. As we rowed away he stood on the strand and waved us off with his handkerchief, an oddly incongruent figure on the rocky landwash.

Back on board the *Dove* the first sight to greet me was Froggat, sitting on a keg and drinking from the scuttlebutt. I was speechless for a moment but soon recovered my voice. "Friday! By all that is real, I hadn't expected to see you up! Why, not an hour ago you were lying as still as death."

In my joy I caught him by the hand and pumped it with more vigour than was prudent, for he quickly pulled away and reached for more water. "How are you feeling, my friend?" I asked. "Is there anything you want? Food or—"

I was cut short by the sudden look of anger he turned upon me. It pierced me to the heart, and although I was taken aback I reasoned that he was still in the throes of his illness. In an attempt to disarm the moment, I said, "Perhaps sleep is what you have need of, my friend. Though you must not become an Abraham de Movrie."

I laughed but the hostile stare did not waver. "De Movrie?" I prompted. "Surely you remember that we studied his theorems. He was the trigonometry master who slept longer and longer each day until, on the day that he slept twenty-four hours, he never awoke again." I laughed again, hoping the memory would revive him.

Even as I watched, his eyes lost their fire as quickly as it had appeared. They seemed to glaze and turn flat, becoming devoid of all thought or emotion. It was clear to me that my friend was far from recovered. I placed a hand upon his arm and said, "Friday, you are not well. Let me help you to your hammock."

"No!" he cried, pulling away from my hand as if it carried the plague. "No more! Get away!" His pupils were dilated with fear. His voice was as thin and strained as a sickly child's.

"You have been down with the scurvy, my friend," I pleaded. "Your constitution is still unsettled. Please do me the favour of resting, if only for a while."

I looked him in the eye and doubted whether he saw me at all. Small beads of sweat had broken out on his forehead and his hands trembled like halyards in the wind. I was about to call for help in getting him into the hammock when the voice of Lieutenant Cartwright came sharply to my ear. How had he gotten alongside the *Dove* without being seen? Then I remembered that Grimes had the watch.

"I see that Mister Froggat is up and about," he said, his voice betraying his disappointment. "And only just in time. I had intended to order him ashore before we sailed." He paused and I saw that he was looking at my friend more closely. "Though perhaps I may do so yet."

It can only have been a reflex from his years of service that caused Froggat to stand at that moment and offer a bow. It was the automatic salute of a man who was not in his senses but it was enough to weaken the lieutenant's suspicion.

"Very well then," he sniffed. "Perhaps he will do after all. Mister Squibb, I am expecting Mister Cousens with his Red Indian. As my second-in-command, you will accompany me to the interview, so step lively if you please. And bring your hat and sword. We must impress upon this savage the importance of our mission."

I was relieved that John Cousens did not possess the character that I might have ascribed to him, were I to judge the man by his appearance alone. On any given day the Bedlam Hospital is able to turn out its inmates in more conventional attire. The lieutenant had gone to great lengths to ensure that he and I were presentably dressed, while Cousens seemed to have taken pains to ensure that he was not. He was wearing one, and possibly two, woolen caps topped by a shiny hat of mink's fur, the earflaps of which stuck out at right angles from his jaundiced face. Two or three coarse woolen shirts were layered onto his narrow frame and these fell to the tops of his canvas boots, which were tied above the knee. All worn in the oppressive heat of August.

This odd appearance was enhanced by a long clay pipe that protruded from beneath a nose of equally generous proportion. He took the pipe from his mouth only to speak, while the smoke encompassed his head like a tiny patch of fog. To his credit, Lieutenant Cartwright acted as if there were nothing unusual in all of this. He made our introductions without expression, and proceeded to deliver a long-winded discourse on the purpose and plan of our expedition. Cousens appeared to listen and stared back at us through the haze of smoke.

When the lieutenant had finished, we sat in silence, expecting a response of some kind. We sat thus for several minutes before the man raised his hand and took the pipe from his mouth. We fixed our attention upon him in full expectation of an utterance, but when it came it was only an ambiguous grunt. Clearly he was not disposed to conversation generally, which forced the lieutenant to address the matter more directly.

"I was hoping, Mister Cousens, that you might be of some assistance in our endeavour." He was not to be so easily drawn out, however, and Lieutenant Cartwright continued: "In fact, sir, I had hoped that you would be kind enough to assist us in finding the Red Indians."

Still nothing. The cloud wreathed in an easterly flow, orbiting the yellow face and the hat of mink's fur. The lieutenant cleared his throat in the silence and I knew that we would have to pose a question or else we would sit there all day.

"Mister Cousens," I said, "The governor and Mister Cartwright would be deeply in your debt if you would arrange for a guide to take us into the interior by way of the River of Exploits. Are you able to do that for us, sir?"

The question seemed to have the desired effect, as he removed the pipe from his mouth and looked around for something to spit in. Seeing nothing appropriate in the tidy parlour, he swallowed reluctantly and turned his gaze on us.

"I am able, sir. But am I willing? That is more to the point."

Lieutenant Cartwright looked to me before he replied. I

was well enough acquainted with him to know that he was barely keeping his composure.

"Yes, I take your point, Mister Cousens. Of course the Crown will compensate you for your trouble and expense—"

"Keep your money," came the response.

The lieutenant reddened but said nothing.

"What I require," Cousens said, "is something that you cannot provide."

"And that would be?"

"A guarantee that I will not lose my life by assisting you in such a ridiculous undertaking." The pipe returned to his mouth and the cloud thickened.

The lieutenant flared and bristled, as well he might. I didn't care for the man's tone, either, though I was curious to hear him out. Before Lieutenant Cartwright could muster an answer, Cousens was pointing the stem of his pipe at him.

"Have you any idea, sir, of what you are inviting by going up that river?"

The lieutenant was not given a chance to reply.

"Only one white man has ever gone past the great falls and lived to speak of it. The river is the domain of the Red Indians, sir. Do not push them more than they have already been pushed or we will all pay the bloody *hayoot*."

The lieutenant looked to me and I shook my head in reply. "Pay the what?" he asked.

"The *hayoot*—the devil, sir, in the language of the Red Indian."

I listened to this exchange with a returning sense of unease about our expedition. Threats and warnings have little effect upon my resolution, but I had been harbouring doubts about this scheme since our first misadventure off Bonavista and I could see no reason for renewed optimism now.

"Mister Cousens, our purpose is a peaceful one," the lieutenant was saying "I am not about to 'push' the Red Indians, as you put it. I have come to make a lasting peace with them. And I cannot do it properly without local knowledge. I would not wish it upon my conscience, sir, that our venture failed for want of a man to assist us."

The planter sucked his pipe furiously until I could barely make out the shape of his hat. He said nothing and it appeared that we had momentarily gained the upper hand. The two men locked eyes until I felt compelled to break the silence in the room. "Mister Cartwright, I believe that Mister Cousens' Indian is waiting." Some minutes before, I had seen a man peering through the window and he was now pacing outside the door.

"Very well," the lieutenant said. "Show him in. Perhaps he may have some interest in saving the lives of his people." The remark was intended to wound but Cousens did not twitch.

I arose and opened the heavy plank door, allowing a young man to come silently into the room. I gestured that he might take my chair but he shook his head and stood against the wall, his dark eyes moving from his master to the lieutenant. I remained where I stood, which gave me an opportunity to properly assess the first Red Indian I had ever seen.

I do not mean to be callous but Tom June was a great disappointment to me. Although I had no idea of what to expect, it was certainly not a youth of average build in the clothes of an ordinary fisherman. He bore no tattoos or designs of paint upon his face, nor was there a feather or bead about his person. Moccasins did not adorn his feet and I saw no evidence of a tomahawk hidden beneath his clothes. In the course of my naval career I had heard many tales about the various tribes of Canadian Indians that had fought alongside the French in the last war. These had coloured my expectation and led me to expect nothing less than an Iroquois warrior equipped for battle.

The lad who now stood before me was unremarkable in appearance. His long black hair was tied behind his head, just as I wore my own. His eyes were brown and widely set, and would have imparted a depth of thought or feeling but for their cautious, continuous shifting. His cheekbones were a trifle high and his skin was a shade of light copper, and yet we had Welshmen aboard the *Guernsey* with similar features. He said nothing but his dark eyes missed nothing, even as Lieutenant Cartwright stood up and spoke.

"Would you care to introduce us, sir?"

The planter removed his pipe and said with a sour note, "He knows who you are."

His composure under strain, the lieutenant lifted the tails of his coat and sat down again. "Very well then. Does your man speak the King's tongue or must you interpret?"

"He speaks it well enough. And he understands more than you'd think."

"Yes, let us hope so. Mister June, my name is John Cartwright, lieutenant of His Majesty's Britannic Navy."

The man gave no indication that he'd heard or understood, even as the lieutenant began to explain his mission. I wondered if Tom June had not adopted his master's taciturn nature. One trait which he certainly shared with Cousens was his impertinent manner, amply demonstrated when the lieutenant asked him to draw a map of where his people might be found.

"Me look like Captain Cook?" he retorted.

The gist of the meeting was that the Indian refused to assist us, either in guiding our party up the river or in supplying information on the whereabouts of his tribe. All we were able to learn was that a large lake existed at the headwaters of the Exploits River and that the Red Indians might be found in its vicinity. The only specific item he volunteered was that his father had kept a campsite in a cove on the lake, northeast of the river. It was little enough to go on but it was clear that we could expect no more. At a nod from Cousens, the boy left the room as quietly as he'd entered.

The planter had been silent throughout the interview. With Tom June gone he freed his mouth of the pipe and looked at the lieutenant. "Do you know the history of my man, sir?" he asked.

"No," Lieutenant Cartwright replied. "I do not."

"Perhaps you would care to hear it. The story may prove instructive to you." His tone caused the lieutenant's nostrils to flare again, though he held his tongue in check.

The Beothuk Expedition

"Tom June was brought to me ten years ago, in June of 1758. For the first year I thought he was mute. It was some time before anyone realized that the child was too terrified to speak, owing to what he'd witnessed. He was brought to me by two Irishmen, but do not ask me who they were. I never knew their names and I've not seen them since. They told me they'd found the boy wandering the shore of the Bay of Exploits, near Charles Brook, alone and hungry.

"They were trying to sell him, you see, and had been up and down the coast, seeking offers. None had been forthcoming and now they were anxious to rid themselves of their burden. I took the child and gave them nothing. I wondered later why they hadn't simply killed him. But I suppose they'd made the mistake of letting it be known that he was in their possession.

"The truth of Tom's history came to me by his own admission when he was ten or eleven years of age. His story was confirmed by the confession of a man named Darby McGinn, who died a slow death in Toulinguet Harbour a year later. On his deathbed McGinn unburdened himself of a trip he'd made to Charles Brook with the two Irishmen who'd come to see me. They'd gone there for no other purpose than to raid an Indian encampment and to steal what furs they could find."

Cousens gave his pipe a few short puffs and looked across the room at us. "They murdered Tom's mother, sir. And his brothers, sisters and aunts. The men were away hunting or else they would have been slaughtered, too. They found no furs of value, just a small boy who might be worth a shilling or two."

He sniffed and looked at his pipe. "Now, supposing it was you or me who was Tom's father. How would you feel about a party of white men travelling to the very heart of your country, where white men had never dared to venture before? Would you not feel pushed, sir? Just a wee bit perhaps?"

The lieutenant did not reply. The expression on his face was, to me, a mixture of shock and profound sadness at what he was hearing. In that instant it occurred to me that John Cartwright actually cared about the fate of the Red Indians and that he wished to save them from such cruelty. It was a side of him that I had not seen before, or one that I had chosen to ignore. Our dealings had led me to dislike him for what I took to be his arrogance and pettiness. Had I been wrong in my judgment? Certainly it would not be the first time, or the last.

"Mister Cousens," the lieutenant said in a quiet voice, "your story should be instructive to both of us, sir. While I have gained a greater understanding of the dangers involved in our plan, surely you see the absolute necessity of pursuing it without delay. The fate of Tom June's family must never be repeated. Never, I say! Can we live with ourselves if we do not attempt to change the course of their history? You must answer me that, sir."

His plea did not fall upon indifferent ears. Cousens stood up and paced the room, smoke billowing in his wake. When he stopped he pointed his pipe at me. "And what say you, young sir? Will you follow this man into an unknown wilderness for the sake of a few heathen savages?"

"I will, sir!" I replied without hesitation. I cannot say who was more surprised, Lieutenant Cartwright or myself "Most willingly," I added.

Cousens took another pace or two and turned to the lieutenant. "Then so be it! I will accompany you. Most willingly, as your man says. All we have need of is a guide, and I will do what I can to find one."

He resumed his pacing and puffing as the lieutenant stood and offered me his hand. There was spontaneous goodwill in the gesture and I accepted it without reservation. He opened his mouth to say something but we were interrupted by his brother George, who must have been listening in the adjoining room. Old Atkinson came behind him bearing a bottle of port and four glasses on a silver tray, and a moment later we were drinking to the success of our noble expedition.

My spirits remained high until that evening, when I was standing on the beach and waiting for Greening and the boat to take me to the *Dove*. I turned at the sound of footsteps on the pebbled beach and was surprised to see Tom June approaching me with a solemn air. I bade him good day and for a moment he said nothing in reply. When he did speak, it was with a forthrightness that took me aback.

"Fancy coat navy man is one big fool," he declared. I gaped at him like a simpleton, not knowing quite what to say. There was no doubt that he was referring to Lieutenant Cartwright and his gold and lace uniform. "Says he'll go to red men and talk. Huh! Crazy *bukashaman*. Crazy white man. They'll kill him quick, like others. More quick, when they see his gold buttons and know he's big fish. Kill you too, even if coat is plainer."

I said nothing.

"English men not all bad," he mused. "Maybe navy man not bad. No matter when all trust is gone. Too many English men now. Steal fish from rivers and starve the people. Kill them dead, no reason. English men greedy."

His gaze wandered across the water. "They call us Red Indians when name is *Beothuk*—the people. They call me Tom when name is *Mogaseesh*—boy of the people. White men bring *Mogaseesh* to Fogo when small, to John Cousens. Long time ago. No going back to the people now. Wearing English men's clothes, eating his food and drinking his rum. Smelling like him. *Mogaseesh* knows he be killed if he goes up the river, just like navy man."

Tom June's eyes locked onto mine for a moment before he turned to go. As he walked away I heard him mutter, "Navy man have wig. Huh! He make good prize. Two scalps."

At first light the following day, before there were signs of life from the merchant's house, I took the *Dove* round Fogo Harbour. I wished to test a new rudder that the boatswain had contrived and mounted, the old one having shown signs of rot at the waterline. Neither Hard Frost nor I was willing to leave such things to chance and so we put the shallop through her paces in a moderate breeze. All was proceeding well until Rundle fouled a sheet, causing Jenkins to trip and nearly tumble overboard. I had the two of them sent aft, where they stood before me like lubbers, I declare. I roasted their ears with a few choice words and sent them forward to man our number two gun.

Lieutenant Cartwright had not thought it necessary to exercise the crew in gunnery. I was inclined to disagree, and therefore planned to drill them during our morning excursion. At my signal the gunner ordered the charges and shot removed from numbers two and four. This was to simulate a misfire and to practise the men in reloading the guns as quickly as possible. The wadding and shot were removed from the barrels without injury, though hardly with efficiency. The auger-like worm was then employed to remove the small cartridge of powder at the bottom of the gun. The whole was followed by reloading, in which a new charge was rammed home, followed by the one-pound shot and wadding to keep all in place. To be done efficiently, the manoeuvre requires each man to attend to what the other is doing. I observed that this was not the case at either of the guns. At number four, Grimes and Greening managed to jam the cartridge halfway down the bore, at number two Jenkins caught one of Rundle's fingers between the ramrod and muzzle. What was so painfully obvious had somehow escaped the first lieutenant's attention: in the event of an engagement we were likely to be destroyed.

Frost, in the meantime, had been tacking and wearing the boat around the harbour in a very light breeze. The wind appeared to be stronger outside the islands and he suggested that it would serve as a better trial for his new rudder. I agreed and we sailed for a channel between two islands with the freshening breeze on our larboard beam. The fishing boats had left for their stations an hour earlier, and so I was surprised to see a vessel entering the narrow reach from seaward.

It was a bye boat, a small craft with a stubby mast, and she was tearing along under full mainsail and jib. I judged it unreasonable to attempt a passage through the channel at the same time and gave the order to luff our topsail. We checked our headway and the boat came on quickly with a single man now struggling to lessen her canvas. He managed to do so in an unseamanlike manner and pointed his bow towards us. Having seen our guns and naval ensign, he likely thought it best to pay his compliments. I hadn't the least interest in him but I responded as expected, hailing and asking his business at Fogo. The man shouted back that he was a furrier out of the Bay of Exploits and that he was bringing in his summer pelts. What's more, he said, he'd been running from an armed French brig since the previous evening.

This news increased my interest, you may be sure. I asked him where he'd last seen the vessel and he replied that he'd lost it in darkness near the south side of Change Islands. Now my heart began to race, for the Change Islands were near enough to be seen from Fogo's Brimstone Head. I questioned him quickly on the number and weight of the vessel's guns and her general disposition, to which he gave answers that marked him for a landsman. Yet I knew that the brig could be none other than the *Valeur*, which had somehow evaded our frigates and was continuing to harass our trade.

The bye boat had drifted closer during this exchange and I took a closer look at the man who was in it. He was dressed in canvas and rough-spun clothes that were encrusted with brine, and he wore a broad-brimmed black hat of the kind favoured by religious dissenters. More remarkable, however, was his face, which might have been quite ordinary but for a feature that caused the eye to linger. On either side of his face, from mouth to ear, ran the puckered white lines of two identical scars. I took no time to reflect upon this, the need to alert Lieutenant Cartwright being uppermost in my mind. We quickly pulled our wind for shore and Greening was rowing me to the beach even before the shallop had anchored. Minutes later I was pounding breathlessly at the merchant's door.

The news, to my great surprise, had nothing of the effect I had anticipated. The lieutenant received it with a purse of his lips and little more. Even when I said that the *Dove* was ready to sail in an instant, he maintained his silence. When finally he spoke, it was with the careful phrasing that I had learned to dread from those who are slow to grasp an opportunity. In the polite parlance of the service, they are reluctant commanders, more concerned with weighing the benefits or repercussions of an action than with seizing the day. I knew his reply before he gave it; the answer was like a white flag flown before the battle has even begun.

In a word, he said that we had no orders for pursuit, to which I answered that our standing orders were to protect the trade of the colony. He countered that we were not equipped to fight an armed brigantine, which was true enough. My response was that we might shadow the enemy and learn his intent, thereby providing intelligence to our frigates. I saw his nose lift at my impertinence.

"You will return to the *Dove*, Mister Squibb," he said in a tight voice. "There you will await my arrival and our departure for the Bay of Exploits. Those are your orders, sir!"

The door closed in my face and I was left to stare at its weathered boards. I made an angry retreat across the potato field to where Greening was waiting on the pebbled beach. His eager expression died with a glance at my scowl and he rowed us to the shallop without a word.

John Cousens

It was not the emotion of Cartwright's argument that swayed me. It was instead the nerve that it touched—a nerve that had lain exposed and sensitive these many years. His words had rekindled the pain, and in a way I was grateful for it, as it gave me the chance to make amends.

Like my fellow men of business, I had come to Newfoundland for one purpose only—to turn a profit on my investment. It has been no easy feat, given the lack of governance and the knavery of my competition. At first I concentrated on my purpose and kept a distance from the many evils, both social and political, that are a curse upon this island. I turned an unseeing eye and an unhearing ear to all that did not concern me and I felt that I was doing no wrong. But after a time my conscience began to trouble me.

When Tom June was brought to my plantation I was quick enough to take him in, if only to ease my guilt. It was the guilt of the indifferent and it has burdened me these many years. I told myself that I hadn't come to the New World to take up a crusade against my fellow Englishmen. In fact I was sympathetic to their complaints at first. They had been harassed and attacked by the savages for as long as anyone could remember. Nets, traps, and tools disappeared in numbers, threatening the ruination of men like myself. But then I began to hear tales of reprisal, of murder so foul that I could no longer ignore my feelings of horror and shame. Yes, they used ten-shilling words like reparation and dissuasion, but then I saw their deeds for what they really were—needless violence and barbarous cruelty for which there is no justification.

Then, over time, I began to see a change in the pattern of these acts. At first they had been carried out at random by angry, frustrated individuals, however cruel they might have been. Soon I discerned another hand at work, one that was more methodical, more systematic and wide-reaching in its destruction. Whoever this is, he remains unseen and unknown to me, even today. And if one man is capable of such a thing, he could not attempt it without a highly placed accomplice to watch his back for him.

I need say no more. Any decent person will understand why I agreed to be a part of Cartwright's mad plan. And mad it was, because not a man amongst us was a woodsman. If we survived the arrows of the Indians it would be a miracle. Against that unforgiving wilderness I gave us even less of a chance. As for Tom, I could not blame him for refusing to help. He was afraid. Whether afraid for himself, for us or for his own people, I could not say. I did not tell Cartwright, but in the fall Tom took his leave of us for weeks at a time and had done so since he was old enough to have a mind of his own. I never asked him what he did or where he went and he never offered to tell me. My men said that he met with his father, though idle talk is all it may be. And yet, I believe he knew more about the state of his people than he was willing to tell me.

At any rate, my more pressing concern was the hiring of a guide and pilot to take us to my plantation at Indian Point in the Bay of Exploits. All of my men were away fishing and I was no navigator, having never been in a boat before my first trip to Newfoundland. I am a man of business and inclined to leave the mysteries of the sea to those who know them best. I was therefore compelled to scour the port of Fogo for someone to guide the shallop, a task that young Mr. Squibb urged me to pursue with the greatest haste. Unlike Cartwright, he and several of the crew were much excited by news of a French brig-of-war cruising nearby.

My search did not take long, as all but one skilled man was away at the fishery. I found this fellow in a lean-to tavern in Bank's Cove, in the shadow of Brimstone Head. He was neither drunk nor sober and the sight of him gave me some reservation. He was short in stature, as lean as a fox, and it was plain from his appearance that he was a furrier. He wore a beaver hat and leggings of tanned hide, and his face resembled those leggings in colour and texture. The tip of his nose was white and bloodless, no doubt from frostbite, and above it were two coal-black eyes set uncommonly close together. He also had a mouthful of fine brown teeth and these he showed me in a sly grin when I addressed him. His name was Thomas Rowsell, a name that I am never likely to forget.

He agreed to my offer, though at a price that was only slightly less than a king's ransom. I tried negotiation, then argument and threats, and in the end we settled on a sum that was only slightly less than he'd first demanded. That evening he came on board and we sailed without delay.

I soon had the measure of this Rowsell. A surly, ill-tempered cur would be a good description. He had not the least regard for those around him and he knew nothing of common manners. He farted, spat and wiped snot on a sleeve or whatever else lay at hand. Once I saw him put a finger alongside his nose and blow something disgusting onto the deck. It was only by chance that Mr. Squibb's back was turned. Had he seen Rowsell defile his boat, he would have thrown him overboard. The young lieutenant was very particular about the appearance and operation of that humble shallop. It might have been a flagship for all the attention he lavished upon it.

As we sailed from Fogo, past the northern end of Change Islands and then south of Bacalhau, I had time to observe the others in our party. I was soon struck by what an odd collection they were. Cartwright and Squibb, the two officers, seemed steady enough but the same could not be said of their midshipman. When awake, this Froggat was strange in his speech and manners and was sometimes taken with a kind of fit. I had no doubt that he was ill and I pitied the lad as much as I eyed him with caution.

He was not the only peculiar hand on board the *Dove*. We had as passengers Mr. George Cartwright, the first lieutenant's brother, and a man of the cloth named Neville Stow. Cartwright was of the country sort, forever bidding his servant to polish his muskets and pistols when he was not firing them at some unsuspecting bird or porpoise. This practice of wanton destruction clearly annoyed Mr. Squibb, and I was somewhat put out by the practice myself. The other gentleman, the preacher, was much the opposite in character and disposition. I have rarely seen a man so nervous upon the water and never one so inclined to hold fast to large, heavy objects for safety. I tried to engage him in conversation only once, a mistake that led to some nonsense about the saving of heathen souls. I began to suspect that he was only slightly less mad than the midshipman.

The warrant officers, Bolger and Frost, were typical man-of-war's men. They were blunt and efficient, though I cared little for the boatswain's handling of the crew. Still, he had good reason to abuse some of them. Two in particular seemed half-dazed much of the time, and the petty officer named Grimes was a proper scoundrel. He took liberties where and when he could and was forever cursing the officers under his breath. He and Rowsell fell in together straight away and I frequently saw them consorting and whispering on the forecastle. Mr. Squibb saw them too, for there was little that escaped his notice on board that unhappy shallop

Jonah Squibb

    In ten hours of fair sailing we came to John Cousens' plantation at Indian Point, near the mouth of the River of Exploits. In that time we saw not a trace of the *Valeur*, and Mr. Cartwright and I said nothing more about it. In fact, we said nothing to each other at all. As fractious and disagreeable as he was, our pilot knew the waters well and guided us without incident through a starlit night. I followed our progress by chart, keeping the watch and making notations of my own when he called for a change of heading. I might have engaged him on the finer points but the man was so repugnant that I could scarcely bear to be civil.

    The base for Cousens' enterprise was a large and well-maintained fishing room on a fertile peninsula. There were many flakes for drying salmon and an expansive garden with a variety of vegetables under cultivation. A log structure served as housing for his fishing servants, but as they were all at sea, it made suitable quarters for the crew. Cousens himself invited me to stay at his small house with the Cartwrights and Reverend Stow, which was kind of him, but I decided to remain on board the *Dove* with Froggat. He did insist that I come to dinner, and I arrived that evening to a feast of roasted caribou, sea ducks and the bounty of his garden.

    Old Atkinson had prepared the meal, though the compliments at table were directed to his employer for retaining such a resourceful man. George Cartwright informed us that Atkinson had been with him since the war and had defended his baggage in the hottest battles of the European campaign. When peace arrived the servant had travelled with him to a posting in Minorca and had nursed him through a bout of malaria. Without the attentions of his loyal man, he avowed, he would certainly have perished.

Throughout the conversation Atkinson shuffled unheeded around the table. If he was conscious of being discussed he did not show it, and instead busied himself with removing plates and filling glasses. The excellent meal was enhanced by several jugs of claret that were drawn from a small cask, the very one that I'd put aboard the shallop when we parted company with the *Guernsey*. Toasts were proposed to my foresight, as well as to Cousens' hospitality. The jugs were in constant motion between cask and table and before long Reverend Stow bade us drink a bumper to the King. The others pushed back their chairs and stood as best they could, while the first lieutenant and I remained seated, as was our privilege as naval officers.

It being a Saturday, we also drank the toast of the day—to our sweethearts and wives. The mention of loved ones had little effect upon the good cheer of the company, though my own spirits began to slip. The wine and the toast had once more turned my thoughts to Amy Taverner, which in turn caused a melancholy humour to settle upon me. She was the only girl I had ever loved and I began to dwell upon my loss and the cruel hand that fate had dealt me. I believe I would have become maudlin had the lieutenant not stirred me with a shout.

"Mister Squibb!" he cried. "Come, sir, do not fall asleep on us. We must have a toast to the Navy and you are the very man to do it." He turned to the others and said, "Mister Squibb has quite a reputation for phrasing a toast. I have heard it said that he nearly provoked a duel with a marquis once, over an adaptation of Hogarth's verse."

The others shouted their approval and pounded the table, forcing me from my dismal turn of mind. I stood on slightly unsteady legs and the party fell silent.

"To the King and his Navy," I said. To cries of "Hear! Hear!" I raised my glass: "*Where e're thy Navy spreads her canvas wings, homage to thee and peace to all she brings. The French and Spanish when thy flags appear, forget their hatred and consent to fear.*"

"Hear him! Hear him!" they cried, and there was much cheering and thumping of the table as we drank off the wine. Mr. Cousens asked me whether the lines were of my own composition, but before I had the chance to reply we were interrupted by the Reverend Stow.

"Certainly not, sir," he declared. "They possess the grace and metre of having been penned by a poet, not by a man whose passion is yards and canvas and the like. I ask you, where is the poetry in a pitching, leaking ship? Can anyone answer me that?"

Our ecclesiastical guest had taken too much wine and his tongue was getting the better of him. He gestured for Atkinson to pour and the servant discreetly allowed him half a glass. I ignored the chaplain and answered Cousens, saying that Edmund Waller had composed the verse more than a century ago.

Lieutenant Cartwright, his mind still lingering on the chaplain's comment, looked to him and said, "Come now, Reverend Stow. Surely you have been witness to things of beauty in the maritime world."

"I will admit, sir," the chaplain said with a slur, "that one's perspective of church spires or the buildings of a town may be enhanced from the sea. Otherwise there is little enough of beauty in a ship. The seagoing life would stink in my nostrils if I did not steep it in claret." He took a draught of wine and added, "The Navy and all who serve in her may go to—"

We were never to know what Reverend Stow intended to say. A knock came to the door at that moment and the distraction caused him to spill wine over his waistcoat. Atkinson glided to his side and dabbed it with a cloth while I rose to answer the door. On opening it I found the gunner standing on the tiny porch, his battered hat in his hands.

"Mister Bolger," I said. "Is anything the matter?"

"Oh no, sir. Well, aside from Mister Froggat having another spell, that is. Went all funny and shaky again, he did."

I was reaching for my hat when he added, "Though he's all of a piece now, sir. And sound asleep." An awkward moment followed and I guessed there was another purpose to his visit.

"Is there anything else, Mister Bolger?"

"Aye, as a matter of fact there is, Mister Squibb. We was wondering—Hard Frost and me, that is—we was wondering if the men might have an extra tot o' grog, sir. We wouldn't ask 'cept the men will likely have to go without when we leaves for the wilderness."

I considered this a moment and said, "I see no reason why they shouldn't. You have my permission, Mister Bolger."

"Who is it, Mister Squibb?" the lieutenant called from the dining room.

"The gunner, sir."

"What does he want?"

"He was asking about extra grog for the men, sir. I've told him—"

"Yes, by all means!" Mr. Cartwright said. "The men must have their grog. Allow them what they wish, in honour of our last night in civilized surroundings!"

I did not think this prudent but it would have been less prudent to argue the point.

"Well, there you have it, Mister Bolger," I said, "But I hold you responsible for them. Especially Grimes. I have forbidden him any spirits, as you know."

The gunner's blue-flecked lips drew back in a grin and he jammed the hat on the shiny dome of his head. "Never ye worry, sir. Me and Frost'll keep an eye on that bugger."

He knuckled his forehead and turned to go, and then suddenly slapped his thigh. "Oh, sir! I nearly forgot. A man showed up 'bout an hour past. It were the damnedest thing—just tied his boat up alongside the *Dove*, he did, no more to it than that. Says his name is Sam Cooper. He's one them of furriers and him and Rowsell knows each other. Can't say I cares fer the look of him, but then I don't care fer the look of that Rowsell, neither. And, sir, tis the strangest thing but this Cooper is the same—"

A summoning cry from the lieutenant cut him short. The gunner quickly took his leave, fearing that the lieutenant had changed his mind about the rum. I returned to the room where Reverend Stow looked as if he were still at sea and having trouble controlling his stomach. But at least he'd stopped talking.

"Ah, there you are, Squibb," Lieutenant Cartwright said. "Have another glass." Our strained relations seemed to have been forgotten in the flow of wine.

I accepted the offer and caught the eye of our host. "Mister Cousens," I said, "a man named Cooper has sought shelter in your outbuilding for the night. He says you will have no objection."

"Cooper?" he said. "Not Sam Cooper?"

"Yes, I believe that is the name."

Our host fell silent as he fingered his glass. "Well, well," he said a moment later. "Gentlemen, Mister Squibb tells me that we have a visitor. It is none other than Sam Cooper, arrived here at Indian Point." The rest of us looked at him without comprehending.

"This is the man I was telling you about. Sam Cooper is the only one to have ever travelled past the great falls on the River of Exploits."

Lieutenant Cartwright and I exchanged looks. Such a guide would be worth his weight in treaties with the Indians.

"Then we must have a word with him," the lieutenant said.

"Is he trustworthy, Mister Cousens?" I asked.

"I cannot answer that, as I barely know the man. But his employer certainly is not. I believe that Andrew Pinson's sharp practices are well known to yourselves and the governor. That man would trade his soul for a profit, and buy it back at less than the devil paid for it. As for Cooper, all I can say of him is that he is said to be extremely devout."

"Devout?" George Cartwright exclaimed with a drunken grin. "A devout furrier?"

"Why, yes," Cousens replied. "I recall my men saying that he is a man of extreme religious conviction."

"A companion for our dear chaplain, then." George Cartwright laughed.

The lieutenant and I looked at each other again. A Pinson man or not, as a guide he sounded too good to be true. "I believe I shall have a word with him," I said.

"Yes, yes," Cousens said. "But first, let us drink another toast of this excellent claret. Will you not join us in a bumper, Reverend Stow? Reverend Stow? Are you quite all right, sir?"

I slipped away a short time later and strolled across the clearing to where the crew was quartered. I opened the door and found the bunkhouse in lively form, with the gunner playing a tin whistle for all he was worth and Frost matching him on a concertina. The instrument looked like a child's toy in the boatswain's massive hands. Greening and Jenkins were dancing a reel and the others were clapping and stamping time.

The music groaned to a halt when I entered the room. Bolger, redder of face than usual and perspiring heavily, nodded to me and said, "Just letting the lads enjoy theirselves, sir."

"Do not let me stop you, Mister Bolger. I am here to have a word with this man Cooper."

"Cooper? Why yes, sir. He's just out there." He pointed across the room to a rear door that opened onto the night. A man stood outside with his back to the light.

"He's a queer sort, sir," Bolger said in a low voice. "Don't seem to hold with rum nor music. But the oddest thing is—"

"Thank you, Mister Bolger," I said, caring nothing for the gossip of the crew. "Please carry on." I crossed the room as Frost squeezed his concertina to life and the sailors resumed their steps. The man who stood outside turned at my approach.

The wine may have played a part, though I believe it was pure astonishment that robbed me of speech. For a moment I could do nothing but stare at the face before me, or more truthfully, at the pair of puckered white scars upon it. It was the very man we'd encountered at Fogo Harbour, which was what Bolger had been trying to tell me. It was beyond comprehension that he should turn up here, and so soon after our first meeting. As I wondered how this was possible, I found my voice and said, "My name is Squibb, third lieutenant of the *Guernsey*. How did you come to ...?"

The furrier's bright eyes bespoke the cunning and quick instincts of a hunter. He saw my surprise easily enough and sniggered before answering in a grating, north country voice. On landing his cargo of furs at Fogo, he said, he'd learned that the *Dove* was on its way to the Bay of Exploits. Intending to return there himself, and having no desire to meet with the French brig-of-war again, he'd followed in our wake for safety's sake. The explanation was reasonable enough, and I went straight to my reason for seeking him out.

"Mister Cartwright has a proposal for you, Cooper. He wishes to hire your services as a guide on the river. You see, the governor has given him the task of—"

"I knows his task," the man cut in. His voice had the quality of a keel being dragged over gravel. "He wants to find the Red Indians."

The crew had evidently told him as much, and so I said, "That is correct. We intend to make—"

"Ye intends to make a truce with 'em."

I merely nodded, avoiding the certainty of further interruption.

"Ye'll be wastin' yer time," he rasped. "They'll hear no talk of peace."

"Why, sir," I responded lightly, "I was told that you are a Christian man. Surely you have faith in the ideal of peace?"

Cooper's bright eyes bored into mine. He said nothing and I sensed that he was turning the question over in his mind, examining it as he might examine a questionable pelt. His nose twitched as if he were trying to catch the scent of it as well.

"And ye wants my help?" he said at length.

"Yes. Mister Cartwright will pay you for your trouble, of course."

"Pay me?" the man said. "Why, tis not honest work he's offering, now, is it?" There was another pause as his tongue flicked over thin, cracked lips. He appeared to be considering the proposal, and at last he said, "All right. I'll guide him, sure enough. But only 'cause the Lord might have some purpose in me doin' so."

"The Lord, you say? Then perhaps you believe the souls of the Red Indians should be saved?" The thought of another companion like Reverend Stow was unsettling.

A sly grin twisted his mouth, and he replied, "Oh, I didn't say that, now, did I, sir?"

Israel Frost

Oh, it were a grand old evening, sure enough. First chance the lads've had to kick up their heels in a fortnight. And when they was all done with dancing the hornpipe, they took to singing the old songs. Bolger give us "Black-eyed Susan," which I never heard these ten years or more. Then Greening sung "Nancy Dawson," which I been hearing every hour this month. I told him to learn something new, if he knows what's good for 'im. I sung one meself, what I learned from the cook on the old *Phoenix*, called "Poor Jolly Sailor Lads." Never heard it, you say? Why, I can sing it again. Ahem—

> *Come all you pretty fair maids, a line to you I'll write*
> *In ploughing of the ocean I take a great delight.*
> *On land you have no danger, no danger do you know*
> *While we poor jolly sailor lads ploughs on the ocean bold.*
>
> *When labouring men come home at night,*
> *they tell their girls fine tales*
> *Of what they been a-doing out in the new mown fields.*
> *Tis the cutting of the grass so short, tis all that they can do*
> *While we poor jolly sailor lads ploughs on the ocean blue.*

Here's the night as dark as any pitch and the wind begins to blow,
Our captain he commands us, all hands turn out below.
Our captain he commands us our goodly ship to God,
Jump up aloft my lively lads and strike topgallant yard.

You see a storm is rising and we are all confound,
Looking out every moment that we shall all be drowned.
Cheer up, never be faint hearted, we shall see our girls again,
In spite of all our danger we'll plough the raging main.

So now the wars are over and we are safe on shore,
We'll sing and we will dance me boys, as we have done before.
We'll sing and we will dance me boys, and spend our money free,
And when our gold it is all gone we'll boldly go to sea.

Oh aye, she's a grand tune. And we had a grand time of it, too. There were no fighting neither, though Grimes and young Greening was eyeing each other. A nasty piece o' work is that Grimes. I seen his like before, mind you. And plenty of 'em. Most don't carry much skin on their backs by the time they been in the fleet a year or two. Which is the only way o' putting the fear o' the Lord—and the bo'sun—into 'em.

Mr. Squibb has other ideas, o' course. Not that I'm saying the young gentleman is wrong in his thinking. Oh no, Mr. Squibb is sound enough, though he don't have much experience in dealing with sea lice like Grimes. Take them few lashes that him and Rundle got from each other. It done the trick in keeping 'em apart fer a few days but it didn't set Grimes to rights, now did it?

Last night I were watching Grimes real close like, 'specially when he thought I weren't looking. I saw from the start how sweet he and that Rowsell is on each other, and now they're after getting a third hook on their line. Who's that, you say? Why, that God-botherin' Cooper, is who. I don't like the looks o' him, I can tell you. And I don't mean them scars. Someone said him and Mr. Squibb was much alike, as they bore their past on their faces. I said that might be true enough but the likeness ends there. Cooper may have somethin' in common with Rowsell, them both bein' furriers and all, but why are they splicing up with Grimes? Makes me wonder. Mind you, I'll be watching 'em closer than a gull watches fer capelin. All the way up the river. You can bet yer last drop o' grog on that.

Jonah Squibb

           At the break of day, on the 24th of August, we sailed the *Dove* from Indian Point to Peter's Arm and dropped our anchor. The two furriers followed in Sam Cooper's bye boat. There we readied the jolly boat and stowed it with a week's provisions, each man to carry fourteen pounds of hard bread and seven pounds of salted beef, together with a share of the weapons, kettles, spare powder and ammunition. If the journey lasted longer than seven days, we would have to hunt for our rations.

    The sky was clear with a light westerly playing outside the arm, but within it we lay in a calm that invited a great swarm of black flies to join our company. This added to the general misery of everyone aboard, myself included, for the previous night's revelry had taken its toll. I was reminded of Fielding's observation that there is nothing so idle and dissolute as a sailor on land. Indeed, Lieutenant Cartwright's mood was not so expansive this morning and the men were generally lethargic. Reverend Stow had lost his breakfast on the trip over and even Frost, an old hand at debauchery, appeared the worse for wear. Bolger looked like death delayed, though I knew he would have put us all to shame in the hardships that lay ahead, had he been given the chance.

As it was, the lieutenant informed him that he was to stay with the *Dove*. The gunner was far from pleased but he had the good sense to keep his lips together. Without further ado we wished him well, and he us, and we clambered over the side and into the jolly boat. It was close quarters, even with the furriers in their own craft. George Cartwright, Reverend Stow and John Cousens each sat between two oarsmen. Froggat took the bow while the first lieutenant and I were jammed in the sternsheets. Our number was twelve plus the two furriers, the addition of Cooper being a relief to the superstitious sailors.

Froggat seemed a good deal better that day, at least in physical health. He showed no signs of impairment in scrambling into the boat, though he was uncommonly quiet. As a boy he had chattered like a magpie, even talking in his sleep at times. Now he sat quietly in the bows, his hat pulled low over his eyes. There he stayed, as silent as the wide river beneath us, as we began our journey into the wilderness.

The men rowed for three hours at a steady stroke and at nine o'clock we put ashore at Jumper's Brook, a good three leagues from Peter's Arm. Here we took a brief rest and a few mouthfuls of bread before carrying on. A short time later the walls of the forest moved closer to us as the river narrowed. At length we came to the salmon weirs belonging to John Cousens and under his direction we navigated the maze of woven sticks and netting. The traps had yielded him several hundred quintals of dried fish that spring, he said, and it had not been his best season. George Cartwright took a particular interest in this and posed many unwelcome questions on markets and prices.

The current grew stronger as we progressed and after much effort on the part of the oarsmen, we arrived at Start Rattle. It was a little before noon when we beached the boats and unloaded our supplies. Each man was given his food and equipment and I armed Froggat with a pistol and the boatswain with a fowling piece. The Cartwrights and Cousens had their long-barreled muskets, as did the furriers. I equipped myself with a pistol and gave the remaining men a hatchet apiece. This brought a complaint from Grimes until Frost silenced him with a threatening fist.

The lieutenant's plan was to divide the party so that we would travel each shore, thereby increasing our chances of meeting with the Indians. He cautioned that we were not to fire our weapons in any circumstance, unless our very lives lay in the balance. This caused a new round of complaints, chiefly from his brother, who was incapable of restraint when a living creature came within range of his gun. With this and other matters settled, we bid adieu to the south bank party, consisting of George Cartwright, Reverend Stow, Frost, Greening, Rundle, Jenkins and Atkinson. The remainder of us—Lieutenant Cartwright, Cousens, Grimes, Rowsell, Cooper, Froggat, and myself—rowed across the river and dragged the two boats into the trees.

The lieutenant took the lead and I brought up the rear. I recall thinking that it was odd to have left both guides on the same side of the river, but in all likelihood Lieutenant Cartwright was not thinking clearly. It seemed unimportant at the time but much later it would have consequences beyond my ability to imagine on that day.

Our progress was very good for the first hour, and our companions on the south bank matched our pace despite a great many boulders and jagged rocks in their path. We had cleared the rattle and the river was running smoothly between us when I looked across and saw much waving and gesturing from the other side. Calling this to the lieutenant's attention, we stopped and I took out my viewing glass, quickly discerning the cause of the commotion. They had come upon a wigwam, or *mamateek*, as Joseph Banks had called it, sitting in a clearing. There were no signs of occupation, but all hands were excited to see that we had arrived in the territory of the Red Indian.

Lieutenant Cartwright and I were discussing whether to return to the boats and cross over when Cooper pointed to something further along our own side of the river. I put the glass to my eye and saw that it was a second *mamateek*. A moment later I spied another, and yet another. All along the bank, for three or four cables, I saw hut after hut. Some had fallen into disrepair and others looked quite habitable. The discovery of so many dwellings quickly changed our mood from excitement to caution. I checked the priming pan of my pistol, as did Froggat, and the men nervously fingered their hatchets.

There was no cause for unease however, as we discovered that the houses had been abandoned for some time. We searched a few of them but discovered nothing of value or interest, although the structures themselves were quite remarkable. Each was of a conical shape, the base seemingly proportioned to the number of people who would occupy it. Inside and surrounding a fire pit were oblong hollows in the earth that Rowsell said had served the purpose of beds. Each hollow was lined with young branches of fir or pine and upon these the Indians would lay their furs. A dozen straight sticks made up the conical frame of the hut and over these were laid large pieces of rind from the birch trees. The pieces overlapped, sheet upon sheet, in the manner of shingles, and covered all but a smoke hole at the top and a small entrance at the base. The rind was secured in its place by other sticks that were laid against the outside of the structure. We lingered long enough to satisfy our curiosity before pushing on.

The rocks on the south bank of the river became larger and more troublesome as we progressed, until the party under George Cartwright had difficulty keeping pace. The day was wearing on when we came to another set of rapids that our guides called Little Rattle. Here we found a hut of a different design—being in the shape of a rectangle instead of a cone. It was framed nearly in the fashion of an English house, with wall studs and a sloping roof of rafters. We discovered a sizable frame of sticks adjoining this large structure, on which lengths of split roots and fine sinews were tied. It had all the appearance of a rack for drying salmon, a staple food of the Indians. We also found several arrowheads nearby and a kind of fleshing knife.

I examined these items with interest and they provided me with a perspective that had hitherto been lacking. I began to think of the Red Indians as a more substantive entity, as fellow beings with whom we shared the common concerns of food, warmth and shelter. Here was evidence of creative and resourceful minds at work in the wilderness, and I was greatly impressed. Of course, the same could not be said of everyone else. Rowsell and Cooper showed no concern for anything save the forest around them. They watched the trees like lookouts at the masthead, their guns always levelled in readiness.

It was late afternoon when Grimes began to complain of his feet and stomach. He complained so much, in fact, that I was obliged to speak to him sharply. We were all very tired but we carried on throughout the evening and just before dusk we arrived at what our guides called Sewel Point. This was the limit that any European save Cooper had travelled before. The small outcrop in the river afforded a view of a magnificent falls that roared like thunder a short distance upstream.

At the behest of Cousens, Cooper described his visit here in the company of another furrier two summers before. They had been trapping beaver in the small brooks that fed into the river, he said, and had intended to travel above the falls when they discovered an Indian canoe at this very spot. His companion, who was a new man, feared an encounter and retreated down-river as fast as he could travel. Cooper was not so easily deterred and the promise of pelts drew him on for three more days. He claimed to have encountered no other human being in that time.

There were several huts on each shore below the falls and it was here that Lieutenant Cartwright decided we would spend the night. After signalling our intentions to his brother's party, he and I ascended the steep bank and surveyed the country above the cascade. It was an uncommon feeling to stand at that apex and know that in a few days' time we would look upon a landscape that had never been seen by white men before. I am bound to admit that thoughts of this, and the possibility of other discoveries, thrilled me very much.. As a rule I am not impressionable, but that evening, as we watched the sun set in a narrow band of purple and gold over the wide River of Exploits, I felt something of the grand scope and purpose of our undertaking.

The next morning we were up and moving before dawn and only then did I think to ask Cooper why our campsite was named Sewel Point. He smugly replied that if I had been more observant I would have seen a mile or more of "sewels" on both sides of the river last evening. I chose to ignore his tone and asked him the meaning of the word. He grudgingly explained that a sewel was a tassel of birch rind tied to a stick of about six feet in length. The Indians would then drive these into the ground at some yards apart, so that the rind dangled and played in wind. His explanation was all well and good but it still did nothing to make clear their purpose. When I asked him to explain their use, the furrier was amused at the question.

"They're used," he said, "to catch the eye of what ye intends to kill."

I turned his words over in my mind as we made our way up the river and soon came to understand their meaning. The puzzle was not solved by the power of my reasoning alone, I will confess. Instead we came upon a kind of fence that could only have been constructed by the Indians. Large numbers of trees had been felled, birch and poplar alike, one upon the other in a straight line that followed the bank of the river. Sticks and brush had been added to fill the gaps, along with a number of these sewels.

I surmised that the fence had been built to intercept the caribou as they passed in migration and to force them towards a particular place. This was confirmed when we came to an opening in the fence, situated above a steep embankment that led down to the river. Here the Indians would wait and slaughter their quarry as they passed through the gap. I was struck once more by the ingenuity of these people and their stratagems for survival in the wild.

Our progress that day was not as rapid as either Mr. Cartwright or I would have preferred. Our companions were still having difficulty on the south bank, and we were obliged to wait for them on several occasions. During these delays the two furriers would walk into the forest to explore the many brooks and streams that flowed into the river. They were plainly in search of a new source of pelts and on their return they would scratch little maps on birch bark with the points of their knives. The prospect of profit had done much for their courage, for they no longer seemed nervous of the forest. It was early evidence of a greed that would become much bolder in the days to come.

All that day we passed abandoned huts as well as a cleverly constructed raft and two partially built canoes. What we did not discover were signs that the Indians had been there in recent weeks. Cooper went so far as to say they hadn't been there in many months. Our second night on the river was passed in one of the *mamateeks*, as partial protection from the mosquitoes and blackflies, and by dawn we were walking again. Lieutenant Cartwright was convinced that we would find the Red Indians farther inland, near the great lake that Tom June had described. He became more convinced of this when, on the third day, Grimes claimed to have seen a canoe full of men in the distance. They had been armed and war-like, he said, and I listened to this with more than a little suspicion. No one else had seen them and Grimes was forever complaining of the walking, the flies and the heat. Nothing would have suited him more than to have us turn around and return to the relative comfort of the *Dove*.

Unfortunately for him, his claim had the opposite effect upon the first lieutenant. He became more eager than ever to push on and he drove us hard on the fourth day. The other party was pressed to keep up and twice we lost sight of them for hours at a time. We had been without communication, save for the most rudimentary kind, since the start of the journey. In places where the river had been narrow enough to shout across, the rush and splash of the water had all but drowned our voices.

When I awoke on the fifth morning I looked across the river and suspected that something was amiss. Rain had started during the night and although we were dry inside a large hut the others had not been so fortunate. They had slept under the trees around a campfire that now smouldered in the rain. There was no sign of activity but a scan through my glass found the seven men sitting in the undergrowth, and a sorry-looking lot they were. Some were attempting to repair their shoes, others lay motionless except for listless slapping at the mosquitoes, and all were as wet as seals.

The lieutenant asked my opinion and I said that we ought to establish their condition, which did not look promising. How this was to be done was another matter, for while the river ran smoothly between us, it was at least a hundred yards wide. I said that I would try to find a way across, and leaving my pistol with Froggat, I walked upstream to investigate. Before long I discovered two large tree trunks that had washed ashore. By observing the flow of the river, I concluded that any object launched from this point would make its way to the other bank in the general vicinity of our companions. I therefore placed the two logs side-by-side in the water, straddled them as I would a horse and then pushed myself into the stream. The soundness of my idea was quickly put to the test, and it was not the verdict I had hoped for. The current took hold of my little raft and spun it around like a leaf, propelling me downriver at an alarming speed.

I was clearly in trouble, and I believe I would have drowned if not for some quick action on the part of Greening. Seeing my predicament he grabbed a hatchet and sprang into action. At a stroke or two he toppled a long pole of birch and thrust it into my path as the current pushed me past the south bank. I had the good sense to grab it as I was swept along, losing my seat and tumbling into the water. Others lent a hand and the pole was drawn in to bring me safely to shore. I was soaked to the skin but no worse off than the men who helped me to my feet. They had been lying in the rain all night and to make their misery more complete, most of them were crippled for want of a decent pair of shoes. For all that, Frost and Greening found my antics on the river quite amusing. Greening tried to hide a smile but Frost laughed outright at my sodden appearance, reciting: "*Mother, may I go out to swim? Why yes, my darling daughter, fold your clothes up neat and trim, but don't go near the water!*"

I ignored the jest and turned my attention to the state of their footwear. George Cartwright and Reverend Stow had been well shod to begin with and their boots had stood up to the sharp rocks. The sailors' shoes were another matter. Frost and Jenkins had not a sole between them and they'd walked the last mile in their bare feet. The cuts and abrasions were ugly enough but Frost had also twisted an ankle and was favouring it. Greening, Rundle and Atkinson were not much better equipped, with mere flaps of leather hanging from their uppers.

There was only one course to follow, and there and then I ordered the four sailors to make their way back to Start Rattle. Greening began to voice an objection but I silenced him quickly enough. I heard no word of complaint from Rundle or Jenkins, though Frost alone made up for that. The boatswain was determined to argue the point, even after I had hardened my tone and said the decision was final.

"But sir," he protested, "this here is a naval expedition. With me and the lads turned back, there'll be more lubbers than seamen. Now that can't be right, can it, sir?"

"I believe we can uphold the honour of the Navy in your absence, Mister Frost," I replied.

The grey pigtail hung wet and limp as his small eyes peered across the river and then back at me. I knew what was really on his mind, and it was not the honour of the Navy. "You don't take my meaning, sir. Some of them you're left with can't be relied on. Why, I wouldn't trust 'em—"

"I am aware of their shortcomings, Mister Frost. That is my duty, is it not?"

My tone quieted him but he gave me a seething look. I took him by the sleeve and drew him away from the others. "Listen to me, Frost," I hissed. "With that ankle, you are as useless as a hulk on a lee shore. At least Grimes and the furriers can walk and fire a musket if need be. Now these men must return to the *Dove* while they can. I have my doubts whether they can manage it alone. You must go with them. There is no one else."

He heard me out and nodded his head in resignation, realizing that what I said was true. He would only slow our progress or worse still, force us to abandon him or give up the expedition entirely. Having put the matter to rest, I informed our two gentlemen that they were free to return to the shallop, if they chose to do so. They were volunteers and could not be expected to bear the difficulties that were already multiplying upon us. I had anticipated a particular response from each of them but their reactions were, I have to say, the complete opposite of my expectations. I had scolded Frost not five minutes earlier about knowing the shortcomings of those around me. It now became clear how little I really knew of these people.

Mr. George Cartwright, the bold young army captain, fairly jumped at the chance to retreat. He invented no excuses, I will give him that, other than to say he'd had enough. And yet, the speed with which he gathered his things was remarkable. Without a trace of embarrassment he asked that I convey his regrets to his brother.

I was not fully recovered from this when a second surprise came in the response of Reverend Stow, who declared his absolute determination to stay the course. He spoke emphatically of fulfilling his mission, of finding, as he put it, "those savages who have yet to receive the glad tidings of salvation." Oh, but the poor chaplain was a sorry sight, standing there in the streaming rain with his wig plastered to his skull. He looked at me defiantly, as if I might order him away. The thought hadn't even entered my mind, for how could I deny a man who would endure so much for his convictions?

I suppose I must have looked a sight as well, listening incredulously to this reversal of my expectations. I regained my wits in time to stop George Cartwright as he set off with faithful old Atkinson at his heels. I asked him if he would not give up his boots so that another man might carry on. I think he would have told me to go to hell had the others not been watching. Instead, he sat on a rock and his servant pulled the boots off with difficulty. I picked them up and gave them to Greening, who grinned with delight as he handed the gentleman his battered shoes with their flapping soles.

Derek Yetman

Friday Froggat

It was the sight of poor Jonah struggling in the river that marked the change. I came to my senses just after that, though at the time it felt like I was watching myself fighting that mighty current, trying to survive a force that was far greater than any I could overcome. But just as deliverance and solid ground came to Jonah that morning, so it came to me.

The Lord knows I've had sickness and injury aplenty in my time, but never the torture of mind that had hold of me in those weeks. There were moments when I could think clearly enough, and only then did I know that I was surely going mad. I plainly recollect falling ill on board the *Liverpool*, and being told it was the scurvy. From there it was naught but a hellish nightmare of demons who came to claw at my reason and to tear at my soul. They brought hideous thoughts that were not my own and unspeakable cravings that took possession of my very being. I had fallen into an abyss without hope and was allowed to live only to prolong my suffering.

I recall that Jonah was with me much of the time, and without him I would not be on this earthly plane today. Perhaps it was the shock of seeing him in mortal danger that caused the tide to shift, but whatever it was, I began to make sense of what was going on around me. Mind you, I wasn't sure who some of my companions were, though I recognized Nehemiah Grimes from the *Liverpool*. There was something else about him, too, only for the life of me I couldn't remember what it was.

I wasn't sure how I came to be in the Newfoundland wilderness, either. But that and the other gaps were caulked by and by, thanks to Jonah. He told me everything and right happy he was to see me back in my senses, I can tell you. Lieutenant Cartwright didn't seem to care one way or another. Jonah told him he might have lost five men to poor cobbling but he was gaining one who made the trade nearly even. The lieutenant gave him a funny look when he said that, like he thought it might be a fling against his brother leaving the way he did.

I also found something in the pocket of my old uniform coat. It was a tiny figure like a pendant, carved from bone or antler, I suppose. It wasn't more than an inch long but it was cut real fine in the likeness of a child. I couldn't say how it got there until the memory returned to me by degrees. It was our second night on the river, when we were lying in one of them Indian huts. I was awake in the dark, a fair bit dazed but I recall the moonlight coming through a hole in the roof. It was lying right there in that little patch of light, this tiny figure, and I must've picked it up and put it in my pocket, which is where I found it on my resurrection day.

After that I had a good few things to ponder as we beat our way up the river, especially the nature of the sickness or madness that I'd just come through. Jonah said it was more than the scurvy, which made me think about my time in Bonavista. I couldn't recall much, but for some reason I had the notion that Grimes figured into it. I gave it a good bit of thought and after a while it gradually came back to me. Only by then, it was far too late.

Jonah Squibb

We now found ourselves, Reverend Stow, Greening and myself, isolated from our companions on the north bank of the river. Lieutenant Cartwright signalled for us to continue upstream and this we set out to do as best we could. Boulders and sharp stones contrived to slow our progress until late in the morning, when we came upon a chain of rocks that stretched across the torrent to the other side. It was not for the weak of heart but we succeeded in leaping from one slippery knob to the next, arriving safely to the cheers of the other party.

Lieutenant Cartwright received the news of his brother's departure without a word. I am certain that he was disappointed, but he did no more than cast a hard look at the boots on Greening's feet. That the chaplain had volunteered to carry on must have made his brother's choice doubly hard to bear. In any event, he decided that we would remain as one party, our strength of nine men being too small to risk dividing. We therefore continued our trek until late afternoon, when the rain finally ended and the sun appeared, to the great relief of our minds and bodies. I suggested that we make camp early to dry our clothes and to cook a proper meal, and after receiving reluctant consent we took our well-earned rest in the sun.

I was lying awake as the others slept in the last of the day's warmth when I saw Tom Rowsell sit up and look around him. Seeing no sign of wakefulness from anyone, including myself, he rose to his feet, picked up his musket and powder horn and silently walked into the forest. I thought little of this, assuming that he had gone to relieve himself, when to my wonder, Cooper stirred a moment later, took up his weapon and followed. This was more than a little suspicious, but what they were up to I could not guess.

A few minutes later I was following their trail as quietly as a sailor in the forest can manage. Fortunately the trees were well spaced with thin undergrowth, so that I made little noise and was able to glimpse them in the distance from time to time. At intervals they would stop and listen, casting their eyes back along their path and keeping their muskets at the ready. They led me on in this manner for some ten or fifteen minutes until I observed a sudden change in their behaviour. Their attention was drawn to a noise or movement on their left, and they moved cautiously in that direction, now crouching, now stretching to see, all the while as silent and stealthy as cats.

It took much of my concentration to avoid stumbling or snapping branches, but I followed them as closely as I dared. They were clearly stalking something and from time to time would freeze as still as statues, their ears cocked to the trees in front of them. At such intervals I stopped in my tracks and held my breath, but I heard and saw nothing of what they were fixed upon. After one prolonged pause I saw Cooper gesture to Rowsell, who nodded and moved to his right, flanking an especially dense stand of undergrowth. Cooper remained where he was, slowly standing to his full height and raising the musket to his shoulder. Rowsell, completing a right angle to the cluster of bushes, turned and pointed his weapon into it.

I was now convinced that they meant to fire their guns, in spite of Lieutenant Cartwright's orders. I plunged forward without another thought, dropping all pretense of stealth and making more noise than was strictly necessary. They held their stance for a moment, as if reluctant to look away or to acknowledge my approach. When they turned to face me their expressions were at first startled, then hostile. There was a moment of complete silence as I halted in front of them, followed by a rustle in the undergrowth. Something moved quickly away from us. I cannot say what it was, but as ludicrous as it may sound on reflection, at that moment I could have sworn that it was running on two legs.

Cooper stood before me, choking with rage. Rowsell remained where he was, off to my right, though I could easily see his infuriated face. "What is this?" I demanded. "You know the lieutenant's orders. There is to be no shooting." They stared at me, saying nothing; I could not fail to notice that the muskets were still at their shoulders and pointed more or less in my direction.

"You will return to the river immediately," I said in my quarterdeck voice. Still they did not move or take their eyes from me. I met Cooper's glare and raised my voice, "To the river, man! Now!"

From the corner of my eye I saw Rowsell's brown teeth as his lips drew back in a sneer. The long barrel of his musket drew level with my chest and he inclined his head to one side, as though intending to sight along the barrel. Cooper remained motionless, although the barrel of his musket lifted perceptibly. At such close range the muzzles seemed as broad as the mouths of cannon. Every fibre of my being tensed and I fought the urge to flee, duck or cringe. My pistol was tucked into my belt, and little good it would have done me in defence. In the seconds that followed I swear that I could hear the very worms in the earth, so stretched were my nerves and senses. The air around us felt charged, as with lightning, and the tension as tangible as the sweat upon my brow, when a sharp metallic click intruded upon my consciousness. It was the unmistakable sound of a hammer being cocked, and the sound did not come from either of the muskets that were pointed at me.

Cooper's eyes focused on something behind me and I saw Rowsell lift his head. There was silence again and as I stared into Cooper's face I saw his expression change. The fury did not ebb so much as become cloaked or hidden. To my right, I saw Rowsell's musket waver and dip while the smirk dissolved from his lips. Finally, Cooper lowered his barrel and looked away. Only then did I turn to see Froggat standing some yards away, a pistol in his hand. His face was grim and he kept his eyes fixed on the furriers. The two men walked away of their own accord, back the route they had come from the river, with never a word spoken. My sigh of relief was a welcome one; I had been holding my breath for some time. Froggat uncocked his piece and fell in with me as we followed the treacherous pair.

I was shaken by the incident but I had the presence of mind to thank my friend for his timely intrusion. He said that he had seen all three of us leave the camp and had thought it best to follow in turn. Plainly I was not the only one who harboured a deep mistrust of Rowsell and Cooper. On our walk to the river my mind raced with thoughts of what I should do. That I must do something seemed obvious enough, but the right course of action was not readily evident. That they were not to be trusted was beyond any doubt, but what was to be done about it? My first thought was to report the incident to Lieutenant Cartwright, but then I began to anticipate his reaction. Perhaps I had mistaken their intentions or misjudged the situation, he would say. Had I any proof that they were about to do me harm? Did they announce their intention of shooting me? I had my friend's word as to what had passed, but the lieutenant would have little regard for what Froggat might say.

I could practically hear his voice: "Plainly you startled them as they were about to shoot at an animal. They turned and naturally their guns were pointed in your direction. I see no evidence of menace from what you have related. They may be guilty of wanting to eat something besides salt beef, but little else."

My ears burned with indignation at the imagined conversation until my thoughts turned onto a different track. Even supposing that he accepted that they had threatened the life of a King's officer, what was to be done with them? Placing them under arrest for the remainder of the expedition or returning them to the *Dove* under guard was impractical, to say the least. Short of tying them to a tree there was nothing that I, or anyone else, could have done.

On the afternoon of our sixth day on the river the devil showed his cloven hoof. Grimes had been malingering all the morning and Froggat and I were obliged to shout at him to keep up with the main party. He was throwing sullen looks and murmured curses like a man hard done by and was whining about his feet, which were no more blistered and sore than anyone else's. Finally one of his soles came loose, either by accident or design, and he refused to walk another step without fixing it. He was seaman enough to have a needle and twine with him but Lieutenant Cartwright refused to wait. I ordered Grimes to make his repairs and to catch up as soon as he could.

In hindsight, as is ever the case, I can easily see through the man's deception. He had been by far the most fearful amongst us, forever casting worried looks at the trees and sleeping with his hatchet in his hand. He would not squat in the woods without being able to see the rest of us. The proximity of his bodily noise and stink disgusted us all, even the furriers. With that in mind I should have been suspicious when he raised no objection to being left behind.

As it happened, I was tired and thinking none too clearly. We were all on the point of exhaustion, having marched by my calculation some twenty miles a day under the most trying conditions. I believe that Mr. Cartwright, like myself, viewed Grimes as something less than an asset, especially in his effect upon the morale of the others. We therefore left him with no great reluctance and he watched us go without a word of complaint. The treachery that had been brewing for some days came to a head a few hours later.

We stopped to rest in the heat of midday, and within minutes all hands had fallen asleep where they sat or lay. Half an hour later I awoke with a start, disturbed by the immense silence around me. I looked and counted five sleeping figures, two less than there ought to have been. Cooper and Rowsell were gone, along with their packs and guns, and I had no doubt that they'd planned their flight with Grimes in advance. The petty officer had been clever enough to create an excuse for himself earlier in the day, knowing full well that naked desertion would see him hanged or flogged to within an inch of his life. The furriers, as hired men who did not belong to the Navy, would suffer nothing more than the loss of their pay.

But why would they forfeit their wages? As experienced woodsmen the hardships of the trek had been nothing to them. And I doubted whether they had abandoned us out of fear. Had Grimes offered them some incentive to leave with him? If so, what could it be? I had already established that he possessed ready coin, though it was surely not enough to bribe the others. And what of the man's own greed? I could not imagine him willingly parting with a ha'penny. It was then that a new suspicion became lodged in my mind. It was a vague notion at the time, and one that I could not put coherently, but over the following days it took on form and substance.

I awoke the lieutenant to tell him the news and, to his credit, he said that we would do as well without them. We roused the others and our small party pressed on until later that same day, when we were forced to leave Greening behind. His borrowed boots had all but disintegrated and a small track of blood had appeared in his wake. Normally diffident, he surprised me with his strenuous objections, saying he would walk on his bare feet if he had to. I explained to him, as I had to the boatswain, that he would only hinder our progress and endanger our mission. He relented in the end, but with a pledge to mend the boots and follow us as soon as he could. Froggat was kind enough to leave him his pistol and all of his powder and shot.

That very evening, in the last hour before darkness, our journey on the river came to an end. We were turning a bend in its course with Lieutenant Cartwright leading, when suddenly he uttered a cry and threw up his hands. The gesture occasioned some alarm, as we thought he was under threat. Cousens was the first to come up to him and all concern was dispelled when he threw off his burden and danced a little jig. His laughter and excited hallooing echoed between the rocks and trees.

The rest of us quickly caught up to them and were greeted by a vista that left us awed and speechless. A great lake, larger than anything I had ever seen or imagined, lay spread before us with a surface as smooth as the glass on my compass. The flat calm mirrored perfectly the golden sweep of the western sky, with one half of the setting sun still hovering above a far-off mountain. At the time I thought it the most beautiful sight in the world, and while we stood in silence the sky and its reflection in the lake changed to brilliant ochre as the sun sank behind the distant peak.

We were lame, exhausted, hungry and maddened by clouds of flies that gave us no peace, and yet we were elated. We walked a short distance along the shore in the twilight before choosing a point of land on which to spend the night. Froggat and Cousens set about gathering firewood and Reverend Stow readied the kettle to boil the last of our salted meat. Lieutenant Cartwright made an entry in his journal while I reflected on how our weariness and pain were of such little consequence in the light of our achievement. We were the first white men to look upon this great, nameless lake—the first to witness God's glorious and divine creation. I spent some time in contemplation of the event and was more than a little pleased with what we had accomplished.

The lieutenant was not about to rest on his laurels, however. He soon joined me and began to outline his plans for the morrow, when we would begin our survey of the shoreline. This was certainly the lake that Tom June had spoken of, but the lieutenant was keenly aware that reaching it was not the task that the governor had laid before him. Contact with the Red Indians was uppermost in his mind and I could only respect him for his dogged pursuit of his duty.

We were interrupted in our discussion by an exclamation from the chaplain. He had just realized that the day was Sunday, a fact that had escaped us all in the mind-numbing routine and weariness of our march. He soon had us assembled for prayers by firelight and all present gave thanks to the Lord for the success that we had met with thus far. The lieutenant, in honour of the occasion, officially gave the name of Sabbath Point to the spit of land on which we were camped.

That evening I smoked my pipe beneath a canopy of stars and considered what we had to be thankful for. We were reduced to a handful of exhausted men and we had less than a day's ration of bread to sustain us. We were crippled, bitten, sore and stiff, and not visibly nearer to success than we had been a week earlier. But we were alive and in good spirits, which was something at least. Froggat came and sat beside me after the others had made their beds in the sand. He was like a man reborn compared to the shadow of himself that I'd watched so anxiously since leaving Bonavista. I was happy for him and pleased that we could at last sit in one another's company as we used to do. We savoured our pipes in a comfortable silence, staring at the star-encrusted sky, until I remarked that it was the kind of night a navigator might dream of.

"Do you miss the sea already, Jonah?" he asked with a smile.

"To tell the truth, I haven't been this long ashore since '62, when we were at St. John's with Colonel Amherst. I can also say, without fear of contradiction, that I have never walked so far in my life."

He laughed and stretched a leg to the fire. "And if we were to turn back this minute, we'd still be only half-way to the sea," he observed. "More likely we're not a quarter finished, I'd venture to say."

"You may be wrong there, my young friend. We haven't the food or the feet to go much farther. Lieutenant Cartwright is reluctant to admit it, but he knows the facts as well as I do."

"You don't believe we'll find the Red Indians?"

"I am not optimistic." I picked a brand from the fire and relit my pipe.

Froggat toyed with a small object that looked like a piece of bone. "Tell me about Bonavista, Jonah," he said. "About you finding me there."

"I've told you all I can," I said, knowing that he was still attempting to fill the gaps in his memory. "You were sick and your captain sent you ashore with three of the *Liverpool*'s crew. They left you in the care of an incompetent surgeon and that is all I know. By the by, do you recall a book of Oliver Goldsmith's that I once lent you?"

"Goldsmith? Why, yes. *The Vicar of Wakefield*, wasn't it? Don't tell me I haven't given it back!"

"No, no. But you may remember that the author had once been a surgeon, and not a very good one. After he turned to writing, he told an acquaintance that he now only prescribed for his friends—"

"Oh yes! I remember. The acquaintance replied, 'Pray, doctor, alter your rule and prescribe only for your enemies.'"

"That's it." I chuckled. "Sound advice for the surgeon who attended you as well."

"I can't remember anything about him, you know. I recollect first coming down with the scurvy, on board the *Liverpool*. It's after they took me ashore that it's all confused. And what about Grimes and his mates? What were they up to while I was laid low?"

"Waiting for the *Guernsey*, as they were told to do. And drinking the town dry, from what I could see."

"With what?" Froggat laughed. "Old buttons?"

"Oh, no. Grimes seemed to have a full purse and he was spending it freely enough."

"Really? Fancy that!"

A short silence descended upon us before I said, "But come now, Friday. I've heard nothing of you for a whole year. And I had no idea that you were on board the *Liverpool*. The last I knew, you were on the *Audacious* and in charge of her signals. What has happened since?"

Froggat knocked out his clay pipe and leaned back on one elbow. "Well, it was a memorable year, I'm bound to admit. I joined the *Liverpool* after my last letter to you, just as she was sent to escort a convoy of East Indiamen out of Plymouth. We sailed on Christmas Day, a poor time to sail to be sure, but we

The Beothuk Expedition

rounded the Cape and arrived in the Indies without a hitch or a hangnail. We were there some weeks while the ships went about loading their spices and timber and such. Then in late February we sailed from Bombay and charted a course for Persia, our first stop on the voyage home. It was a routine enough business, as you know."

I nodded in agreement. "Well, that's when it all changed. I was second in command of a prize we'd taken a few weeks before, a corsair that was caught harassing a merchantman. She was local built, though sound enough and we sailed her to the Persian coast in hopes of finding a buyer. While we were there and the Indiamen were taking on a cargo of silks, a fierce storm blew up from the Indian Ocean. What they calls a typhoon in those parts. Well, we had no choice but to run before it and the prize I was on was separated from the fleet. We were driven westwards along the Arabian shore for days on end."

Froggat paused to relight his pipe. "There's a thick haze on the sea in them parts," he resumed, "owing to the heat and the sand storms that comes out of the desert. We had a young lieutenant in command, younger than me he was and be damned if he didn't put us aground in the middle of the night. There was no damage but before we could refloat her, we found we wasn't alone on that desolate shore. A dozen small boats come bearing down on us at first light the next day. They were *dhow*-rigged but they turned out to be a kind of vessel called a *battil*.

"Now your *battil* is not like your other *dhows*—your *boum awas*, *sambouks* and *jalibuts*. *Battils* are speedy little craft that can manoeuvre as smart as ye please and the Arabs use 'em for pirating work. They carry a pair of three-pounders each, which pose no great mischief, but their tactic is to swarm a vessel at once and overcome it. It's easy enough to blow two or three of 'em out of the water, mind you, but before you knows it the rest are alongside and you're boarded in no time at all. That's what happened to us and we'd no choice but to strike our colours in the end. Only the ship's boy and myself were taken unwounded. The others, dead and wounded alike, were thrown over the side. Then at high tide they took the two of us ashore to their stronghold."

There was a long pause in the darkness. I waited until he spoke again.

"Ah, Jonah, it was a cruel, cruel place. The heat was like nothing I ever knew and the sun a scourge upon our heads. We were taken as slaves and joined a gang of others—Persian, Arab, Goan, and the like—that were building a great fortress alongside an oasis. It was the only water for miles around and the tribesmen gave more of it to their camels than they did to us. Oh, there was many a time I wanted to lie down and die, just like those around me who did so every day. But me and my shipmate held on, as did an African we'd befriended who showed us how to survive in that scorching hell of a desert.

"We suffered this for months until the new moon in the month of April. By night we were locked inside the very fort we were building, with its walls of clay and stone six feet thick. Our guards manned the corner towers with muskets and escape was impossible, or so I thought. One night while we lay on the ground with the snakes and the scorpions, I heard the usual call to prayers, which they obey five and six times a day. But then I heard none of the usual praying from the tower nearest to us. When I realized this I made so bold as to stand up, which brought neither shot nor shout from that quarter. It looked for all the world like they'd left us unguarded. I stirred my two companions and we hastened to the base of the tower, where the ship's boy found purchase with his small fingers and toes. He scaled that brick turret like a foremast jack and in no time at all he'd let down a rope to us..

"Well, we were over them walls and into the night before you could say *Allah akhbar*. Turns out it was a feast day, with everyone gathered in the village and our guards not wanting to be left out. They wasn't much concerned about us because we had nowhere to go anyways. If we went into the desert we'd be mad with thirst in a day and dead by the end of the second. And there was no place to hide, the land being as flat and treeless as the ocean.

"On the other hand, we knew there was a boatworks in the harbour and that the shipwrights had just launched a big *dhow* called a *baghlah*. This was a proper ocean-going ship rigged with them big lateen sails. Now, an Arab boatyard is normally a guarded place because of a powerful superstition. They believes that if a childless woman jumps across the newly laid keel of a boat she will conceive. But for every life that comes into the world in this manner another has to leave it, usually that of a builder. Which is why they guard their yards careful-like: to keep the women out.

"All the same, on that particular night everyone was gone to join in the great feast, excepting one watchman. We stole aboard the *baghlah*, and our friend the African wrung his neck as neat as you please. I knew nothing then of sailing such a craft but we soon found our companion to be a seasoned hand. Under his command we slipped away without so much as a shot fired at our stern. Luck was on our side from the start, ye might say, and it carried on with the strong, hot northerly wind until we met with our convoy a week later. Two months after that we were in Plymouth and the *Liverpool* began fitting out for the Newfoundland station."

Froggat drew on his pipe and in the flickering light he appeared to contemplate the ordeal. It had been quite an experience, and although I knew him to be a brave and resourceful lad, it had taken more than that to survive such captivity. I told him as much but he laughed my comment off with his usual modesty. It had taken him months to escape, he said, when I would have managed it in a fortnight.

As I yawned it occurred to me that his recent illness might have been related to his captivity, but when asked he said that he'd been the very picture of health until the scurvy came upon him. We lapsed into silent thought at this until, after a while, he asked if I knew what had become of his sea chest. I said that it hadn't been with him at Bonavista and must therefore have been left on board the *Liverpool*. I cannot say whether he replied to this, for within minutes I was fast asleep.

Derek Yetman

We awoke to a light rain and mist, although the day promised to be tolerably warm. For breakfast we ate ship's biscuit and then set out to explore the northeast corner of the lake. A ribbon of sand between the trees and water made the walking easy and we came to a shallow cove at noon. Lieutenant Cartwright called for a brief rest, during which he wondered aloud if this could be the cove that Tom June had spoken of. His notion was confirmed when we explored further and discovered what had once been a large clearing near the beach. We soon found evidence of an Indian settlement, with new growth overtaking the studded log houses and the collapsed poles and bark of *mamateeks*. Here, as we gnawed the last of our hardtack, the lieutenant named the place June's Cove, which he wrote in his journal. He also voiced his opinion that Tom June's tribe had become greatly diminished since the boy's capture ten years before. Cousens agreed, adding that he'd heard a rumour of the Mickmacks trapping the western end of the lake. They would never have attempted such a thing if the Red Indians had strength in numbers, he said.

We resumed our trek with hunger gnawing at our bellies and I realized with some concern that we had seen almost nothing in the way of game. I also regretted having come away from the ship without a hook and line, for several times we saw large salmon or trout jumping in the lake. After two hours more of marching in the rain we came upon a square house and several *mamateeks* in good repair, but again they bore no sign of having been occupied since the previous winter. Once more we stopped to rest and took out our pipes as a poor substitute for food. It was then, my resolve strengthened by fatigue, that I gave voice to the evidence that was mounting around us.

"It appears to me that the Red Indians have not been here, or even upon the river, in many months," I ventured.

Cousens grunted. "We have seen nothing to encourage us."

The lieutenant looked across the water and scratched his fly bites. "And when did you arrive at this opinion, Mister Squibb?" he asked in a weary voice.

"Several days ago, sir."

He nodded and sighed. "At about the same time that I began to have my own doubts." I toyed with my pipe until he added, "But yet we know that they still exist. Where can they be?" The question was directed as much to the silent trees as to any of us.

I scratched my own bites and said, "I have given that question some thought, sir. And I have come to believe that they are a migrant people."

The lieutenant looked at me in surprise. "Really? Do go on."

"I believe, sir, that they spend their winters here on the lake, travelling upriver from the coast when the caribou migrate. In the spring they go down to the sea, where they hunt birds and salmon and gather eggs for their subsistence."

He smoked his pipe as he considered my theory. "It is plausible. But why did Tom June not tell us this?"

"I can only assume that he didn't want us to find his people, sir."

The lieutenant looked at me askance. "Not find them? Why the devil not? We are here to offer them peace, after all."

"Aye, sir. But he may have seen no good coming of it. He may not have trusted our motives or perhaps he thought the Red Indians would not greet us amicably, and that more blood would be spilled."

"Hmm. You may be right, Mister Squibb. You may indeed. But what of us? A hundred miles or more from our boat without a scrap of food. With hardly a piece of leather to our feet." He lifted a foot and the sole of his boot hung loose. "And to what end?"

"At least we know something more about them," I said, "which will make the task less difficult the next time."

"The next time? Hah!" He sighed and shook his head. "There will not be a next time, Mister Squibb. I fear that we are too late already."

Neville Stow

        The Lord be praised! My little flock and I are safely delivered into the bosom of this strange land. We have faced the trials of the tempter as did Christ himself in the wilderness, and we have kept faith and held sight of our divine destiny. I offer up a prayer of thanksgiving and hope that we will meet with the Red Indians soon, that I may begin the work for which I have been chosen.

        The establishment of the New Heaven will be greatly advanced by the addition of these simple Indian souls. And even those who have already departed this earthly plane will be among their number. Oh yes, it is all part of the grand design, you see. I have come to realize that every savage who has heard the word of the Lord will become the medium by which those who have passed on will be delivered unto His salvation. Think of how quickly we shall populate the New Heaven!

        And I have struck upon another idea that will be certain to please our Maker. The Last Judgment having taken place, we are now reaching out to the unlettered, the untutored and those who were closest to mankind in his natural spiritual state. I have therefore decided to cast the net of salvation wider still and include another tribe in my mission. What tribe is this, you ask? Why, the tribe of Newfoundlanders, no less. They are simple enough from what I have observed and they know hardly more than the Red Indians when it comes to the word of God.

Take the young sailor, Greening. One evening as we were sitting by the fire, he spoke to me in tongues, as sure a sign of the Lord's will as ever there was. His words made not the least sense, and yet I know that he was possessed of a spiritual visitation. He was speaking of Nehemiah Grimes, calling him a *buckaloon*, a *sleveen*, a *tallywack*, and a *bullamarue*. He spoke as well of our party being in a fine *codge* and a proper *hinker*.

What manner of speech is this, I asked myself? It was certainly none that I had heard before. I was puzzled at first and asked Mr. Squibb what it meant. He tried to dismiss it as part of the local dialect, but then a divine inspiration came to me. The Lord had made the man speak in a strange tongue to remove the scales from my eyes! Here before me was a simple soul, reared half-wild in this distant colony, knowing next to nothing of God's intent. And there were many more like him who were, in the final summation, no different from the Indians of the forest.

There will be exceptions, of course. That man Cooper, for one. When I heard that he was a God-fearing Christian, I naturally drew him into my confidence. He did not look particularly devout, I will admit. Fierce would be a better description. With those hideous scars across his face he looked as wild as the creatures he hunted. When I explained my calling to go amongst the Red Indians he had the nerve to say that he, too, had received a message from the Lord. He said this to me, an ordained man of the cloth! I explained that I was seeking the pure of spirit, that they might find peace with our saviour in the New Heaven.

"Pure of spirit!" he mocked. "The Red Indians? They're naught but the devil's servants, put upon this earth to serve their master. And naught but a fool thinks any different." As he spoke his eyes blazed, though not with the light of Christian zeal. The affront left me at a loss for words.

"But you're partways right, preacher," he said. "The Lord will have them. Oh yes, but not on the terms you might imagine.

Derek Yetman

He'll have them as He commands us to deliver them. I have received His message and it's clear enough. To me belongs vengeance, sayeth the Lord!"

Those were the only words that Samuel Cooper ever spoke to me. As much as I regret it now, it did not occur to me that I should tell anyone what had passed between us.

Jonah Squibb

On the evening of the following day we prepared for our return journey to the sea. Mr. Cartwright was dejected and disheartened, and repeatedly expressed his regret at not having a boat to take us across the lake. He seemed convinced that, if we were able to climb the far-off mountain, we might see smoke or other evidence of the Red Indians. It was a last, desperate wish and in the end he had to settle for putting a name to that distant peak. He called it Mount Janus, for the Roman god of gates and beginnings.

We were ready to begin the long trek to the sea when it occurred to Cousens that the lake itself had not yet been named. Froggat immediately proposed that it be called Lake Cartwright. The lieutenant refused the suggestion with great humility, saying we had all shared in the privilege of being the first Europeans to set eyes upon it. Perhaps his reluctance had something to do with the inclusion of his brother in the name, and so I made a suggestion of my own, saying that it ought to be called Lieutenant's Lake, in his honour. He did not immediately protest, and so Reverend Stow declared the lake duly christened, to be known henceforth and always by that name. We sealed the act with a toast of water, and although we were tired and the rain had returned, at least our spirits were higher.

We had nothing to eat that night but it was not the hunger that kept us awake. Wolves had come to the river and we heard them soon after dark, howling and barking from all directions. We lay in the open with our guns close at hand, never daring to close our eyes as we listened to their hideous, mournful baying. They seemed to be everywhere, both near and far, though it may have been a trick of the night and the hills around us. When daylight came we stumbled onward, limbs dragging with fatigue and stomachs growling like the creatures that stalked us.

We had no food that day and spent the night as we had before, lying or sitting awake and listening to the wolves. The next morning Cousens shot a rabbit that we immediately dressed and hung over a smoky fire of damp wood. The rain had not lessened and the smell of roasting meat only made us more aware of our misery. We sat by the fire and shivered in our dripping clothes, knowing that it would be another three or four days before we reached the *Dove*. Our progress was further slowed by Reverend Stow, who was fevered and had taken to mumbling scraps of the Psalms. We were a sorry sight indeed, more savage in our appearance than anything else and also in our manners. When Mr. Cartwright cut the half-cooked rabbit into five pieces we devoured it shamefully, becoming ever more like the wolves that haunted us. The one bright moment in our day came that evening when we overtook Greening as he struggled downriver. He was a welcome addition to our party, though his feet were horribly torn and bloodied.

We began to crave sleep as much as food but to stop for any length of time would have been folly, as we might have starved to death where we lay. And yet, we could not go on without rest. On the third day we found a broad, flat rock in the river that provided some protection from the wolves and we lay down upon it. I was not more than twenty minutes into a troubled sleep when I was awakened by a commotion and a splashing in the water between the rock and the riverbank. I opened my eyes to see Froggat, who was our sentry, waist-deep and losing his footing on the slippery stones of the bottom. The

The Beothuk Expedition

current pulled him onto his back and for a moment only his hand showed above the water, holding one of our precious pistols aloft. A few yards farther on Reverend Stow was scrambling up the muddy bank.

Froggat resurfaced, coughing and shouting and bringing the others awake. The lieutenant and Cousens grabbed their muskets as they sat up, blinking and exclaiming in confusion. When Froggat had gained the shore and recovered his breath, we learned that Reverend Stow was delirious and running amok. Froggat had tried to stop him but the chaplain, like a man possessed, had gotten the better of him. Each of us looked to the forest, where only a rustling and snapping marked our companion's progress through the undergrowth. I quickly proposed that I join Froggat in pursuit while the others remained where they were. Lieutenant Cartwright seemed about to object but I swiftly gathered up my pack and jumped from the rock. "If we haven't returned in one hour," I called over my shoulder, "carry on and we will follow you downriver."

At first we plowed our way blindly through the brush, until I thought it wise to take a bearing from my compass. Having established the direction in which our rock lay we moved ahead more cautiously, pausing now and then to listen for anything other than the ever-present cries of the wolves. The undergrowth was dense and we were soon scratched and bleeding. A little after this we came under close attack from a swarm of stouts that had scented our blood. Froggat groaned that our misery was now complete, but he led the way through the ever-thickening forest.

When next we stopped to listen and to consult our compass, we heard a cry—very faint but unmistakably that of a man. Ignoring the sharp twigs and thorns we thrashed our way forward until we could hear him more clearly. Fragments of words could be distinguished and minutes later we had the chaplain in our view. He was moving away from us, stumbling at every step and his clothes nearly torn to ribbons. At some point he had fallen into a bog and his lower half was black with mud. He had lost a shoe, his wig was gone and he was in full voice. Either his nerves had collapsed or he had lost his mind, for he was singing a hymn and flailing his arms like a choirmaster. My first concern was that the noise would attract the wolves, or some other form of life that was equally as dangerous.

I saw the figure in the leaves just as we were about to overtake Reverend Stow. It was not more than twenty feet from me and almost hidden by a curtain of foliage. I could see the partial outline of a body, or so I believed, for as I stared, the wind disturbed the leaves and the shape was no longer there. The sight had stopped me in my tracks and Froggat came to a forced halt behind me.

"For God's sake," he gasped. "Don't stop now. Let us get him back to the river." He moved around me and caught the tail of Reverend Stow's coat. I continued to stand and stare until I thought I detected a movement. Was it a trick of the wind or had I glimpsed an upraised hand?

"Jonah," Froggat called. "I could use your help. It will take the two of us to manage him."

Ignoring the plea, I moved cautiously towards the shifting leaves, my eyes glued to the spot as I freed the pistol from my belt. Had I checked the priming in the pan? Were ball and wadding still in the barrel? Like a conjuror's trick, the shape had dissolved again. Was it a man? I had a skin of gooseflesh as I reached out and pushed the leaves aside. There was nothing there but more branches and leaves. My eyes searched the forest floor in vain for any sign of a presence as Froggat called to me again. Should I tell him what I had seen, I wondered, or had I in fact seen anything at all?

My friend was urging the reverend to stop singing, and after another lingering moment I joined them. My presence seemed to calm the poor chaplain, and he smiled at me as if we had just met on a stroll round the quarterdeck. He hummed quietly to himself as we led him back to the river. Our journey from that point was slowed considerably, and after we met up with the others we had both the preacher and Greening to help along. The rain had not lessened and the river spilled its banks, forcing us at times to walk farther inland through the trees. We had nothing to eat on the third day or for most of the next, until I chanced that evening upon a large salmon trapped and splashing in a rocky pool. My first instinct was to jump on it before it escaped, for I could have eaten it alive. Reason prevailed, however, and I called the others to consider how best to capture it.

Froggat proposed shooting the fish with his pistol but I reasoned that the ball would refract in the water and miss its mark, and we had no desire to frighten the salmon into the river. I regretted not having a cutlass to run it through and it was then that Cousens suggested the method of fishing used by the Indians. A long, straight pole was hurriedly cut and to this we bound a knife with a strong cord, so that in a few minutes we had fashioned a spear. The fish was neatly impaled on the first attempt and it took all of my strength to hold the pole as it thrashed and threatened to cast itself into the river. Greening had already started a fire and the salmon was little more than warmed before we cut it into equal shares, unable to wait a second longer. How wonderful such a thing can taste to a starving man! And for a few hours it gave us strength, though it was more spiritual than physical.

That night we slept where we were and the next morning, as I roused myself for another tortuous day, I looked more closely at the pool in which the salmon had been trapped. Only then did I notice the stones that had been carefully laid, one upon the other, to keep the fish imprisoned. It was the work of human hands, I had no doubt, and my first thought was of the wraith-like figure I had seen the morning before. Could that mysterious presence have left the salmon for our sustenance? Was it a gesture of peace or compassion for our famished state? It was impossible to know. Perhaps it was a practice that the Indians employed for their own benefit, and we had merely stumbled upon it. All I can say is that it likely saved our lives, for we would not have been able to walk another mile without it.

But walk we did, the whole of the fifth day until we shot two ducks on the river and nearly drowned ourselves retrieving

Derek Yetman

them. We ate as we had before, impatiently and with little ceremony. Even Reverend Stow had ceased his humming and tore into his food with as much rapacity as the rest of us. That night we slept a little, our hunger appeased for the moment, the rain having lessened and the howling of the wolves becoming more distant. We were less than a day from Start Rattle and I prayed that some of the crew would be waiting there. Otherwise we would not have the strength to row ourselves to Peter's Arm.

We awoke to fog, a sure sign that we were nearing the coast, and by noon Greening swore that he could smell the sea. By mid-afternoon we could hear Start Rattle and a short time later we rounded a bend in the river and came upon a peculiar sight—a kettle hanging high up in the leafy green of a birch tree. It was suspended from a limb that overhung the bank and the soot had been carefully washed away so that the polished tin could be seen up and down the river. This was, we soon discovered, exactly the intent of the person who had placed it there. It was the kettle that Sam Cooper had been carrying.

Samuel Cooper

The Lord works in wondrous ways. No truer words was ever spoke. Take this providence that was laid before me now. The Lord put it in my reach, knowing I'd make the most of it. He surely did. But why would the Lord do such a thing for Sam Cooper, you might ask? Because He wants Sam to be the master of his own fate, is why, and be free to walk the path of the Almighty. And what does Sam have need of, to become his own man and follow the word of the Lord? Why it's plain and simple—he needs hard coin. It's hard coin that buys a man his freedom, and nothing else.

Merchants like Pinson pays us furriers in kind, with grub and traps and the like. Or rum for those who'll take it, and the devil's wages it is, too. We're slaves to them and their rum, our feet tied and never free to walk the path of righteousness and freedom. We can never leave this heathen place, but go on living in the woods like animals to make Pinson and his protectors rich. And we're always watching for them savages, watching all the time, lest the treacherous servants of Satan catch us unawares.

Oh yes, a man needs ready coin and to get it he got to make the most of what the Lord puts his way. The Almighty told me that. Told me straight out, He did. "Sam Cooper," He says, "you wasn't put on this earth to be a slave to the likes of Pinson." That's what He said. He also said I had to make the most of what He sends, which is why a man's got to have his wits about him, so he can grab the chance with both hands when it comes along. I knew I had that chance when I got to Fogo a fortnight past. Oh yes, as soon as I heard about the governor's reward I was back on the water and chasing that shallop. This is it, Sam lad, I said. Keep your wits about you.

And that's what I been doing all along. Keeping me wits and calculating me moves. And soon that hard coin will be mine, though first I had to get rid of that sinful Grimes. It was easy enough, I only had to tell him he'd hang for a deserter if he didn't go back. I told him we'd meet up later to share the reward, and off he went. Ha, ha! The Lord works in wondrous ways. Oh, He does indeed.

Jonah Squibb

     The Indian woman had been dead for several days. She lay face down in the brush beneath the shining kettle, a neat round hole through the back of her skin dress. The rocks beneath her were dark with dried blood and I held my breath as I gently turned her over. The natural putrefaction was well advanced, but I judged her to have been of child-bearing age, slim and rather tall. Her long, black hair hung loose and red ochre stained the flesh that remained on her forearms.

     The process of decay was terrible enough, but nothing to the hideous mutilation. Her hands had been severed at the wrists and her face had been disfigured by what could only have been a very sharp knife. The butchery made me think of Joseph Banks and his journal, which I had read at Fogo. The naturalist had heard of similar outrages but dismissed them as nothing more than rumour. Now the terrible proof lay before our eyes. And if that were not enough, her final indignity had been provided by the wolves, which had eaten a good deal of her flesh. Young Greening retched in vain behind me, there being nothing in his stomach to lose. The others stood in silent horror, their exhausted faces twisted with the pain and strength of their emotions. That their fellow man could do such a thing was too unnatural, too loathsome to comprehend.

The girl had dragged herself a short distance after being shot, no doubt hoping to gain the sanctuary of the trees. Whether she had been dead when the knife pierced her flesh was impossible to say but I prayed to God that it had been so. I removed my neckerchief and covered her face before organizing the others in a search around the body. It took some moments for them to move and when they did it was with the dazed and wooden steps of men afraid of what they will find.

Froggat was the first to spot the footprint. It was the outline of a boot heel in a dried patch of mud. Nearby was a second imprint from a man's skin boot, much like that worn by Thomas Rowsell. And then there was a third. It was so insignificant that I failed to see it at first, but there was no mistaking the tiny mark of a child's bare foot, lightly embedded in the damp sand. I called Lieutenant Cartwright and he stared in dismay at the indentation. I estimated the child's age at no more than seven or eight years and when I said as much the full import of what he was seeing struck home. Grasping at false hope, he ventured that the child might have escaped into the forest. Escaped to what, I wondered aloud, with hungry wolves all around? In desperation he tried again, saying that other Indians might have fled to safety with the child. I could not share his optimism, if that was the word. There were no other footprints.

John Cousens finally put voice to what each of us was thinking—that Grimes and the two furriers were responsible for this atrocity. Cousens blamed himself for having recommended them in the first place. It was the remorse of raw emotion, felt by each of us in our own way. The lieutenant said nothing and was like a man turned to stone, crouched beside the tiny imprint with a fist pressed to his forehead. A moment passed before I spoke, saying that the blame lay only with those who had committed the crime and that it was now our duty to bring them to justice.

"But what of the child?" asked Reverend Stow. The shock of our grisly discovery seemed to have moved him to greater awareness. He may have been the only one amongst us who could not conceive of the worst. "Surely they would not kill such an innocent?" he said.

No, I thought, perhaps they would not. The prize would be far too valuable. Another morbid silence fell over us until Froggat intruded upon our dark thoughts, saying that as long as we lingered we lessened our chances of catching the murderers. He was right, but what were we to do with the body? We had no digging tools and we were too weak to use them if we had. Even the moving of rocks to cover her was beyond our physical ability. In the end we could only ask the chaplain to say a prayer for her departed soul, wherever it may now be. We stood with bared heads while he recited the burial verse from memory: *"Blessed are they that mourn, for they shall be comforted. Blessed are the meek, for they shall inherit the earth."*

During the prayer I looked up at Lieutenant Cartwright. Sorrow and defeat weighed heavily upon his features. He had the look of a man whose spirit has been crushed, leaving him devoid of the fire and determination that had carried us so far on so noble a purpose. I bowed my head, unable to look into the face of his despair.

"Blessed are they which do hunger and thirst after righteousness, for they shall be fulfilled. Blessed are the merciful, for they shall obtain mercy." Greening, bless his soul, could not keep from weeping. Even John Cousens ran a finger across his eye. Froggat and I had seen far too much pointless death to feel anything beyond anger and the desire for quick justice.

"Blessed are they who are persecuted for righteousness' sake, for theirs is the kingdom of heaven. Blessed, too, are the pure in heart, for they shall see God." The leaves whispered softly in the treetops, like nature's choir in the church of God's creation. The tall, white birch trees encircled us like solemn mourners, each a reverent and silent witness to what had passed below. The river played its endless hymn for all to hear.

Before we departed I sent Greening aloft to bring down the kettle. That it was placed there to attract attention I had no doubt, and in that final hour of our march to the sea I could think of only one thing—Sam Cooper's answer when I had asked him the purpose of the sewels, those tassels of birch that the Indians had hung from the trees. I heard his voice as plainly as if he were with me, saying they were meant to catch the eye "of what ye intends to kill."

John Cartwright

    My state of mind cannot properly be described; I do not have the words for it. I am now convinced that the men who perpetrated this evil deed were those whom I myself had hired to be our guides. And to make it all the more disheartening, I suspect that one of our own sailors was an accomplice to the crime. I have no proof of this but there is little doubt as to where the compass points.

    The events that followed our discovery of the body have done nothing to lift my spirits. We came upon Nehemiah Grimes at Start Rattle, full of deceit and swearing that he had descended the river alone. I did not believe him for an instant, especially in light of the question that he put to me soon after. Men of his kind are never able to conceal their greed and so he asked me, as bold as day, how the reward of £50 might be claimed for a live Red Indian! God forgive me but I nearly struck him down.

    As for the furriers, our returned crew had seen their bye boat sailing down the bay days before. I have not been able to determine why Grimes was left behind, but I will wager that it is a part of their scheme. Lacking real proof of the man's involvement, Mr. Squibb put the question to him directly. He received nothing for his trouble but blasphemous denials, for Grimes swears that he saw nothing of the furriers after he parted company with us. Still, I am convinced that Rowsell and Cooper have the child and that they plan to collect on Captain Palliser's reward. Whether they intend to include Grimes in the spoils is a question that must occupy the petty officer a great deal.

But in the name of Heaven, how were we to know that it would come to this? I am in anguish at the thought that our noble intention could be exploited in so base a manner. My heart grieves to think that they could have murdered and kidnapped for the money alone. Had I not seen it with my own eyes I would never have believed that such cruelty was possible. I have instructed Lieutenant Squibb to pursue the culprits without delay, as they may yet be caught if no further time is lost. To better serve this purpose I have given him command of the *Dove*, while I remain at Toulinguet with my brother to await the *Guernsey*.

It was my duty to inform Mr. Squibb that he has no legal basis for the arrest or detention of the furriers. They have broken no laws and all previous attempts to prosecute such cases have failed. Governor Palliser has drafted a proclamation but London has yet to act upon it. And so Squibb is tasked with reclaiming the child only. He has been given a free hand to do what he must, even if I have little hope of his success. There are a thousand coves and rivers along this coast that will hide a boat, and these villains are able to disappear into the forest at will.

So there the matter lies. The expedition that was entrusted to me has failed, and in so spectacular a manner that I wonder at what the governor will say. Nothing can put it right, not even the unlikely possibility of Squibb apprehending these men. It will not alter the fact that I have gone to the very heart of this island without laying eyes upon a live Red Indian. To say nothing of making peace with them. And the reward that we have been trumpeting along this coast has now become an enticement to further violence. It is no less than the fruit of a poisoned seed that we had so carelessly planted. Mere words cannot describe the darkness into which my heart has descended. The devil himself could not have engineered so perfect a disaster, nor so complete a humiliation.

Jonah Squibb

I regret to say that much time was lost in convincing Lieutenant Cartwright of my plan. I believe his objections lay more in giving me command of the *Dove* than in the merit of swift pursuit. Every moment of delay jeopardized our chances of finding the furriers and rescuing the child, and it was not until John Cousens intervened on my behalf that he relented, and even then, reluctantly so. Under duress he also agreed that Grimes should come with me, for I had reason to believe that the facts of his involvement would be made clear when we caught up with Cooper and Rowsell. I was convinced that Grimes knew the truth of what had passed on the river. Whether he had knowledge of where the furriers had taken the child was more difficult to say, for I suspected them of intending to cheat him. The rest of the crew believed that he had been complicit in the crime, and if that were not enough, they soon had another reason to despise him.

We found the *Liverpool* frigate departing Toulinguet as the *Dove* entered the harbour and we bespoke her as she was gathering way. Her master was on the quarterdeck and he said they were still searching for the French brig, which might have been a phantom for all they had seen of her. Froggat asked after his messmates and was told that all were well and that the news of his recovered health would be well received. He also asked the master if his sea chest had been put ashore with him at Bonavista. The man said that it had, most assuredly.

It was the answer that Froggat had suspected. Six months of his pay had been in that chest, which did much to explain where Grimes had gotten his ready cash. I took it upon myself to question Jenkins and Rundle on this, and they were mute and evasive by turns. I could see the guilt in their eyes, however, or in Rundle's case, in his one good eye. The warrant officers were all for flogging the truth out of them but I resolved to bide my time. I would wait for proof, both of this and of the far more serious allegations against Grimes. As for Froggat, I was able to convince him that justice, like a good meal, is best enjoyed after some anticipation.

Despite my earlier suspicions of Rundle and Jenkins, I took note of their shock and revulsion on hearing of our murderous discovery on the river. However deeply they were under the influence of Grimes, I was certain they had no prior or later knowledge of that evil deed. Another matter that consumed me was the information imparted by Mr. Cartwright that Cooper and Rowsell could not be tried for their crimes, whether I returned them in chains or not. Incredible as it sounded, they had broken no actual laws. My reaction was astonishment, followed by bitter disgust to know that the beasts of the field enjoyed more protection from the Crown than did the Red Indians. Contempt for those in authority would not help the kidnapped child, however. I would deal with the furriers when I found them, but for now the immediate concern was the chase and how we were to go about it.

The only thing I knew with certainty was that they would head to a large settlement and attempt to collect the governor's reward. Any merchant or justice of the peace would pay them at least £25 on the knowledge that Mr. Palliser was offering twice that sum. Finding them before they sold their hostage would be the challenge, and a difficult one. I would push shallop and crew as hard as they would bear, but first I had to decide in what direction they had fled. The simple answer was east, given that nothing existed to the west save an occasional fishing station. But what route had they taken? They would have to keep out of sight as much as possible and yet stay close enough to shore to escape inland if the need arose.

These considerations pointed to a channel called the Reach, which lay south of Chapel Island and into Hamilton Sound, which was itself south of Fogo Island. If this was their course, I had the choice of sailing in direct pursuit or going north around the island and meeting them as they emerged from the channel. But if I chose the latter, I would have no way of knowing whether they had already traversed the passage or were still in it. On the strength of this alone I shaped a course southwest after we cleared North Toulinguet Island. My decision to take the Reach was a cautious one but I knew that we could easily overtake the smaller vessel in a day or two. The wind was in our favour, being northwesterly for a time, and then veering true west near evening.

We had no passengers for this voyage. The Cartwrights, with Atkinson, had elected to await the *Guernsey* and Reverend Stow was in no condition to carry on. Mr. Cousens had been obliged to return to his plantation, his servants being neglectful of work when left on their own. He was not pleased to leave us but in the end we parted company with many good wishes. We were eight in number on board the *Dove* and all hands were employed as lookouts from our first day at sea. Grimes was useless, of course, and Rundle and Jenkins were little better, having lapsed into one of their peculiar states where they seemed deprived of their senses.

It was Greening who spied a fishing room on the south side of Chapel Island that first evening. I ordered up the jolly boat and he and Frost went ashore to make an enquiry while I waited impatiently. They returned with news that was both good and bad; the fishermen had seen a bye boat heading east two days before and considered it strange that it hadn't called on them. They were uncertain of the number aboard but thought it was either two or three. The less welcome news was that the craft had been under a great spread of sail.

I swore up and down on hearing this. They had somehow jury-rigged the little boat with extra canvas, which meant they were travelling faster than I'd estimated. With two days' lead we would need to set every sail ourselves to overtake them before Bonavista or Trinity, or even Bay de Verde. But in speed lay the danger of bypassing them, especially at night. With this in mind I ordered the jib and topsail set but the mainsail taken in a reef, to keep ourselves in check. My discretion was not solely due to the thought of missing our prey. I was also concerned about sailing an unfamiliar passage in darkness, even with Mr. Cook's chart safely stowed in the cabin.

That night I learned that the Reach is subject to strong currents and variable winds. The shallop was set to heaving and swaying at the most awkward angles and there was little sleep for anyone on board. Part of the crew worked to trim sail and to keep the cargo from shifting, while others kept watch on our course and the shore to either side of us. When dawn came we were as good as worn out, though Froggat managed to rally the men and they stayed alert throughout the morning.

Shortly after six bells we sailed out of the channel and rounded Cape Farewell for Hamilton Sound. Right away, the gunner spotted a vessel anchored in Dog Bay and we came off our course to investigate. It turned out to be a fishing craft with half a dozen men hand-lining for cod. On being hailed, the boatmaster answered that they'd seen a vessel the previous morning. It had been off Ladle Cove at the far end of the Sound and bearing east. This new information gave me pause to consider. The bye boat had been two days ahead of us yesterday and now only a day, which meant they were either heaving to at night or were travelling slower than I'd thought. I dismissed the second possibility as unlikely and focused on the first. If they were putting up at night and we were not, there was a chance that we might overshoot them in darkness.

Tired as I was, I managed to calculate the distance that lay between the two vessels and the time it would take to cover it. I concluded that we would carry on as far as Anchor Brook on the Straight Shore and drop our bower at dusk to wait out the night. I was guessing that the furriers would be doing the same in the region of Cape Freels, some five leagues farther along the coast. If we were underway in the hour before dawn we could, with just the smallest measure of luck, surprise them at first light. Froggat thought my plan a good one, although the warrant officers urged me to press on. They were as impatient as I, but there was nothing to be gained in haste.

Anchor Brook was marked on my chart as a good place for watering, with favourable anchoring ground and some shelter from the sea. We came into the small cove as dusk descended and I sent the jolly boat ashore to fill our casks. The wind had dropped with the sun to give us a still night under cloudy skies, the white semi-circle of sandy beach being all that we could see around us. I divided the crew into two watches under Frost and Bolger and gave them particular instructions to prevent any man from going over the side. They said they would shoot Grimes with great pleasure, should the need arise.

The night passed without incident and we set our sails just as a band of light touched the horizon between cloud and sea. The westerly that had favoured us until now was backing to the south. Under mainsail and jib we cleared Deadman's Point and kept the weather gauge of Outer Cat Island until full light was upon us. I had the tiller while Froggat glassed the shoreline from the poop and Greening did the same from the masthead. We saw nothing before the North Bill of Cape Freels nor had I expected to, though once around the point I thought our fortune might change.

We rounded the Bill and an archipelago of tiny islands unfolded before us, any one of which could have hidden a boat from view. My hope had been to see the bye boat with its sails up and running, but my optimism faded as we moved among the bald rocks. If they were not under sail and were lying hidden in some tiny cove, they would be nearly impossible to find. I ordered our canvas reduced and threaded the *Dove* between Pinchard's Island and the Bight of the same name, resisting the fear that I had miscalculated the speed and distance. Every possibility occurred to me, even that the furriers had kept offshore, perhaps as far out as the Cabot Isles. All hands kept watch as we moved south into Bonavista Bay, although not everyone hoped that we would find the object of our chase.

We were east of Flowers Island and I had nearly conceded defeat when Greening hailed the deck from the masthead. I looked and saw him point southeast, where a small boat was just visible at the rise of the swell. I called for a glass and Froggat put one in my hand. There, in the centre of the magnified circle, was the bye boat, running swiftly under billowing canvas. Frost let loose our reefed mainsail without my order and the shallop sprang to life on the starboard tack. Her lee scuppers went under as we flew over the foaming bay. I was elated and relieved, knowing that it was mere boatwork from here on. The furriers were bound to give up when we brought them within range of our guns, any one of which would wreak havoc upon them.

Grimes began to show signs of increasing nervousness as we closed the gap. He chewed his lip as if it were a piece of salt beef and then took to gnawing his fingers. I was certain that the furriers would implicate him in their crime, a testimony that Grimes feared as much as I welcomed. We were minutes away from coming within range of our prize when Greening shouted again from the maintop. "Sail away!"

"Where away?" I demanded, even as I looked to see his arm stretched to the southwest. All hands turned to see a brigantine, hull up and bearing down with full canvas drawing. She had neither the cut nor the speed of a merchant vessel and I handed the tiller to Froggat as I steadied myself for a closer look. Her large square sails filled my glass, her bowsprit piercing the crests of the waves. She flew no ensign and as I watched, she yawed slightly, revealing four gunports on her starboard side. Just then the ports flew up to expose the barrels of her four-pound guns. From his vantage above me Greening saw what I already knew. "Mister Squibb," he bawled. "She's the Frenchman! She's the goddamn Frenchman!"

The *fleurs-de-lis* ran up the halyard and I ordered Froggat to fall off the wind immediately. He did so and pointed our bow northeast with the wind on our stern quarter. I called for Greening to let loose the topsail and then told the gunner to ready our small arsenal. Our swivel guns were of little consequence against the brig's four-pounders but we would at least make a statement. I was not about to submit to a French vessel, no matter what she could throw at us. Neither, of course, was I eager to do battle with a ship that was more than twice our size and could throw eight times our broadside weight in shot. But I risked court martial if I allowed us to be boarded without a fight and so I instructed Froggat to put us into the lee of Flowers Island. The heavily wooded islet lay a cable's length away and a few degrees to larboard. Our pursuer was gaining rapidly and through my glass I could now see the name on her bows. It was the *Valeur*, and with her mass of sail she would be upon us in minutes.

Flowers Island came athwart and at my word Froggat threw the tiller over and put the wind abeam. The *Dove* trembled and hesitated for an instant before shooting ahead like an arrow out of a sling. The manoeuvre put us into the lee of the island but with enough momentum to carry the shallop along its length. I looked back and was encouraged to see that the brig had not managed to come about nearly so well. There seemed to be confusion on her deck, as if ship and crew were not working as one. The effect of this was the loss of her speed, which was further reduced when she cut across our wake and came into the lee of the island. The *Dove* had by then reached the wind on the other side and was beating southward as eager as you please. At my word Greening had taken in the topsail and Frost had set the staysail. Froggat, meanwhile, played the shallop like a master at the fiddle, bringing out all that she was capable of giving. His fine seamanship gave me time to think on our situation, which was moderately improved by the evasive action.

All that could be seen of the bye boat now was the top of a ragged sail in the southeastern swell. My first instinct was to follow, until sense prevailed and I realized the Frenchman would catch us in a twinkling on the open sea. My only option was to keep a southerly course into the bay, where the many islands, large and small, would provide us with a chance of escape. How quickly the tables can turn, I thought. One moment we were the cat, and the next, the mouse. I looked astern and saw the brig rounding the island and again I was struck by how slowly her crew brought the vessel to bear. Bolger and Frost were watching as well and the gunner declared that she carried a green crew, without a doubt. I had the same thought, surmising that half her complement of two dozen men were likely fishermen pressed from the French shore. Frost murmured, seeming to have read my mind: "*Her four and twenty sailors that stood upon the decks, were four and twenty white mice with chains about their necks.*"

And there could lie our salvation, I dared to think. An unseasoned crew was a great advantage to us. I brought out the chart and considered what lay in our immediate vicinity. My finger traced the maze of rocks and shoals before I gave Froggat a compass heading for Greenspond and its satellite islands, some five or six leagues away on the northwest shore of Bonavista Bay. We would slip through the channel there, I thought, and carry on south to Indian Bay.

As luck would have it, the Frenchman gave up the chase as we put the Greenspond Islands behind us. He had no stomach for pursuit in close and shallow waters, it seemed, and by dusk we were safely hidden inside of Lewis Island. The men toasted our success with a half-pint of rum and water and even Grimes was in high spirits. Plainly his mood had more to do with the escape of the bye boat than with our own good fortune.

I told the crew that we would await the dawn and take up the pursuit again, even though the furriers were certain to make Bonavista before us. They might succeed in selling their captive there, I said, and if this were so we would recover the child and carry on. I swore that we would chase them to St. John's if need be, a statement that met with a hearty cheer. As it died the gunner spoke up, asking if what he had heard was true, that the furriers had broken no laws and were unlikely to be tried or punished for what they had done. His question silenced the company and all eyes turned to me.

I had no desire to lie to them, nor did I wish to dampen the spirit that was driving them on. I answered that it was true that no law existed, but it was equally true that Mr. Palliser would not allow such a crime to go unanswered. He would find a way, I avowed, to bring this evil to justice. Was he not a post captain, governor of the island and commodore of the squadron, all rolled into one? Did he not have the power of life and death over all of us? The men listened and nodded their agreement. The law was a vague and fickle entity in their experience; it was officers and rank that controlled life at sea. They returned to their rum in good humour, confident that the right course would be taken in the end. I saw Froggat staring into his mug and knew that he was not convinced by my rhetoric.

When morning came I sent Frost and Greening onto Lewis Island, to a ridge from which they could survey our surroundings. They returned with news that the air was clear in every direction and that the Frenchman was nowhere in sight. This was enough to convince me that we could make a dash for Bonavista. I laid a course that would take us straight across the bay, a decision that I had no reason to regret as the day wore on. We made good seaway with the wind on our quarter and never a sign of the French sloop, though I hardly dared breathe until we tacked to enter Bonavista Harbour.

Here our luck ran out, for not a soul had seen the furriers or their boat. I could only conclude that they'd skirted Cape Bonavista in the night and carried on southeast to either Trinity, at the top of Trinity Bay, or to Bay de Verde, at the top of Conception Bay. It was the turn of events that I'd been afraid of, and which now unnerved me with the choice I would have to make. It was not the tactical aspect of the decision that filled me with a stew of emotion, but rather the spectre of confronting my past. Trinity was forever in my mind equated with Amy Taverner, and to go there would mean revisiting and renewing the pain that I had tried to suppress these many years.

Now, as we departed Bonavista, my demons were awakened and I was as fearful as a cat upon the sea. I was paralyzed by indecision at a time when the life of a child, perhaps the fate of an entire people, lay in my hands. I was all too aware that the captive's return and the arrest of the furriers might bring an end to hostilities with the Red Indians. An example might be made to both sides, proving that we desired nothing so much as peace and would spare no effort to secure it. It was a responsibility that I would have borne well enough, had it not been for the fear that I would choose my course without the benefit of impartiality. I had every reason to avoid Trinity and I found myself searching for reasons why Bay de Verde would be the better choice.

In the end I decided that if I could not lay claim to logical thought then I would ask the opinion of another. It was a simple but important choice and Froggat was more than equal to it. He immediately grasped that the time we would save by proceeding directly to Bay de Verde would be worthless if they were indeed at Trinity, and the assurance that they were not there would be invaluable to the remainder of the pursuit. His counsel settled my mind, if not my stomach, and at seven bells in the afternoon watch I ordered us south without delay.

On crossing Bonavista Bay earlier that morning we'd made about seven knots with a southwesterly breeze. I was wishing for more of the same, even if we had to beat our way into it after the Catalinas. But it is bad luck to wish for anything, as sailors often say, and they were right enough that day. The wind backed and all but disappeared when we were just a few leagues beyond the Cape. Fog rolled in and during the remaining hours of daylight we made little headway, darkness finding the *Dove* only abreast of the Catalinas. It was a maddening pace, just enough to make the sweeps impractical and yet so slow that we wallowed along like a barrel with wings. The wind did improve overnight, and all that time I paced a tight little circle on the stern deck with Frost at the helm. The men took turns in their hammocks but few of them slept. There was a general anxiety that Cooper and Rowsell were slipping further from our grasp.

Finally at dawn we came to Skerwink Head and drifted into the harbour of Trinity, a tiny vessel emerging from the fog with a crew of hollow-eyed phantoms. The town was not yet awake when we let slip our anchor off Admiral's Rock. We might have tied up at any one of the stages on shore but if the furriers' boat were in the harbour, I wished to keep it there. We commanded the harbour entrance from our position and no vessel, however small, could enter or leave without our knowing. The inside waters were extensive, with two principal arms and a number of coves in which a boat might hide until the chance came to escape. My nerves were by then stretched to their limit with everything that lay on my mind. I bade the men have their breakfast but I took nothing myself, save a pipe and a glass of grog. When they were done and the town had come to life, I ordered up the jolly boat and Greening rowed me ashore before the numbing effect of the rum wore off.

Amelia Taverner

I swear on George Toope's grave that I didn't know him at first. The women and me, we all seen the boat with the navy flag in the harbour when we went to turn the fish. We was all talking about it, the younger ones wondering if there'd be any handsome sailors to come ashore. I paid them no heed, what with having to keep an eye on young Ethan and all. I wondered if they was finally come to do something about them scofflaws and ruffians that's been making our lives a misery. Then someone said there was an officer coming ashore, over by Uncle Benjamin's boatworks. I looked up and seen this tall, skinny feller stumbling out of a rowboat. One of the girls said it's no odds then, if they's all like him. Everyone laughed, and we got on with the fish.

A bit of time went by and then we seen this man again. He was walking the path above the landwash and coming towards our flakes. I could see he wasn't near so old as we first thought, but he looked a rare sight. Right out of Revelations, he was, like one of them four horsemen, he was that drawn and deathly pale. His hat and blue coat was nearly white with salt and I seen better shoes on a beggar man. And then there was that strange scar around his eye, like a cobweb.

He kept his head down as he come along, like he didn't

want anyone to look at him too close. I was bent over with an armload of fish when I realized who he was. Bent over with me head raised up like a goose and me eyes gone round as beach rocks. I couldn't believe what I was seeing and I just stood there while he passed along. I was too stunned to say anything, and wouldn't know what to say if I could.

Lord above, if it wasn't Jonah Squibb, after all these years. And still handsome, even if he did look like a scarecrow escaped from the garden. Oh, how it all come back to me then, all in a flood. How young we was and how much I missed him after they took him away. He blamed Uncle Benjamin for it until Reverend Lindsay, his guardian, put him right about what happened. It was the captain of the *Hector* who did it, pressing a young lad like that when he had no business dragging him off to sea. It near broke the poor reverend's heart and mine, too. Uncle Benjamin was pleased enough about it, what with me being so sweet on Jonah and him being a poor orphan and all. But I didn't care. I was a young maid and I was in love. He might have had the arse out of his pants for all I cared.

I waited three years for that boy to come back. I'd get a letter now and again, even though I wrote to him nearly every week that passed. I know there's always letters going astray and all, but near the end of the third year his letters stopped coming altogether. I knew there was something wrong and it had to be one of two things—either he was dead or he didn't care about me anymore. Either way I was gutted and I thought I'd never get over it. Not in a million years.

But life goes on, don't it? One day I decided I had to pick up the pieces and that's when I said I'd marry George Toope. He was a good enough man, though he was a drinker and not much use to a woman, if you take my meaning. It was a miracle that Ethan come along in that first year but there was no more after that. Which was just as well, 'cause he up and died of the scarletina the second year we was married.

Oh sweet Lord, Jonah. If only you knew how much I cried when you left and how I kept on crying even after I was married. I kept telling myself that you was dead, just to make it easier, and after a while I believed it. Why didn't you come back? Why didn't you ever write and tell me you was alive? I can still feel the pain of it, just like it was yesterday. Only now I'm mad as a hornet, too. How could you do that to me when I was just a girl? I would've run away with you, gone to sea or anywheres else. I would have done anything just to be with you.

And here you are, six years after I gave you up for dead. Smouching around the harbour like some thief caught out in the daylight. Yes, by God, I'm mad. And why shouldn't I be? I want to know why you treated me like that. And why you never came back. I want you to know what I suffered because of you, to see what my life is like now, working the flakes from dawn till dark until I can't straighten my back. A widow at twenty-four with a young one to feed and care for. When I could have been your wife. When I could have been the happiest woman alive.

Jonah Squibb

On our second day at Trinity, long after the melancholy sun had risen, I lay awake and considered all that was wrong with the world. I pondered in particular on the nature of human greed and how it is the cause of so many ills in our society. Wars were fought because of greed, and entire nations called to arms on the chance of gain. Countries were ravaged and civilizations laid to waste because of it. And then there was the smaller scale, the level at which greed destroys the soul and begets an indifference to compassion and even to life itself. It was greed that killed the Indian girl and it was greed that had set us against the Indians to begin with, in our avarice for furs and fish and our outrage at losing a trap or a net. It was greed that had kidnapped the child and it was greed that had sealed his fate.

I had spent the previous day making enquiries around Trinity and had pieced together the sad and sordid tale. Reverend Balfour was the last I'd called upon, and he confirmed that the furriers had arrived in Trinity the day before us. They had an Indian boy in their possession and were attempting to sell him for a fraction of Mr. Palliser's reward. Many were horrified to see so young a child in captivity and had refused to countenance the offer. Others, shrewder perhaps, had refused on the suspicion that the child was too young to serve the governor's purpose. None had thought of paying the money to rescue the poor creature. In the end a buyer was found: an English captain who was leaving for Poole that very day with a cargo of number one fish. By the time we'd arrived at Trinity his ship was twenty hours gone and pursuit in the tiny *Dove* was impossible. The captain planned to show the boy to the rabble of Poole for a penny a head, or else he would sell him to a collector of New World curiosities.

Sam Cooper and Thomas Rowsell were gone as well. They'd sold the bye boat to a fisherman in Northwest Arm and were last seen walking into the woods with nothing but their muskets and their blood money. Where they were bound, no one could say, and none took the news harder than Grimes, who had been outwitted by his partners in crime. One lesson I had learned from all of this was that a greater greed will always seek to destroy a lesser one.

In the evening I returned to the shallop with the news and all hands took it badly. Bolger urged me to pursue the Poole ship at once but even he knew how pointless it would be. There was another course of action that was on the minds of the crew and it was Frost who gave voice to it. He said that the blackguards might still be followed and seized, and made to answer for what they'd done. I said nothing as a murmur of agreement spread across the deck. In truth, I had been struggling with that question since leaving Toulinguet. Yes, they ought to be hunted and brought to justice, but what justice awaited them? They had broken no laws beyond those that govern us as moral beings, and judgment of that would only come from Heaven itself. Not even Captain Palliser had the power to try them, despite what I'd told the men, and if previous attempts were anything to judge by, I knew they would never be convicted.

There was another option, of course. It had come to me early on but I'd pushed it from my mind as too reprehensible, too shameful to even consider. Now the foul possibility raised itself once more and I pondered again the pursuit of the two men, though not with the aim of arresting them. Who would ever know, aside from the two or three trusted men who would accompany me? Who would ever say a word against the deed, even if the truth became known? That they deserved to pay for their crime was beyond question. What lay unanswered was who possessed the moral authority to act upon it.

A heated debate had broken out among the men as to what should be done. Froggat stood behind them, saying nothing and watching me closely, and as I met his eye I knew that he was following my thoughts. I also knew what he would say: to kill Cooper and Rowsell would make us no better than themselves. What did any one of us possess, in the end, but his own honour and convictions? To lose them would reduce us to the level of those we despised. "Silence fore and aft," I said, and the men fell quiet. I heard my voice, strangely distant, fill the void. "The chase is ended. We will pursue no further."

The shocked hush was broken by sighs and groans. I held up my hand. "Our orders were to recover the child. This is no longer possible, and we are obliged to return to the squadron. A report will be made and the boy will certainly be found in England." The men shook their heads, doubtful and disgusted that it all should end this way.

"Listen to me," I said. "Who amongst us is fit to chase these villains through the forest for days, even weeks? Some of you have no shoes, for God's sake. Frost and Greening, neither of you can walk properly with those injuries to your feet. Bolger and Jenkins, are either of you a match for a man who has lived his life in the forest? Are you able to follow his trail? And what will you do if he turns the hunter instead?"

I saw a couple of nods and some shuffling of feet and knew they were coming around. I sealed the argument by pointing out that the furriers could not hide in the woods forever. Sooner or later, they would be found. With that I instructed Froggat to break open the rum. There was no more grumbling and before I went to my hammock I locked Grimes into the fore cabin for his own safety. I retained hope that in time he would face a court martial, and I wanted no man to cheat the hangman.

Derek Yetman

That night an image of the child came into my dreams, based no doubt on what Reverend Balfour had told me. It was of a boy no older than seven years of age: thin, dirty and frightened. He was so tired that he fell asleep wherever he was allowed to stop. The furriers threw him scraps of dried meat from time to time, which he devoured with a hunger that was shocking to see. They had stripped him bare and used an alder switch to drive him before them. The image clung to my mind as I awoke and the dawn turned to day. It was the perfect picture of the greed that I had been reflecting upon, and I knew even then that I would live with it for the rest of my life.

I found my feet and left the cramped cabin, emerging into the purple, melancholy light of dawn. A day of breathless calm was revealing itself and from deep within the bight a loon gave its haunting cry. The crew was stirring with murmured oaths, the results of last night's indulgence now upon them. I did not begrudge the men their drink or the solace they found in it. There had been no joy or music—just the muted voices and lengthy silences of a wake. They had drunk with bitterness and disappointment as their companions and now they awoke to the company of empty failure.

I ducked my head into the wash barrel and held it there, hoping to flush away the image of the frightened child. It did clear my head a little, enough to remember that the boat and crew were still my responsibility and my first duty of the day would be to replenish our stores. We were down to the last of everything and our hunger and exhaustion had not abated since our ordeal on the river.

I released Grimes from his cell and sent him with Froggat and Jenkins to Lester's stores, instructing them to procure what we needed. I put the rest of the crew to work in readying the vessel, with the intention of putting to sea as soon as the shore party returned. I did not have long to wait. They arrived in the jolly boat within the hour, laden with the usual casks and sacks of dried and salted provisions. While they were being stowed, my friend and I filled our pipes and sat on the stern. We said little, but after a time he remarked that he'd seen a large joint of mutton at the merchant's storehouse. It was a pity, he said, that we lacked the means of roasting it on board the shallop.

The mere mention of mutton set my mouth to watering. I also thought of the effect that such a meal would have upon the morale of the crew. Over the last few days there had been much wistful talk of fresh meat, potatoes and sleep. In an instant I convinced myself that time was no longer of the essence, and a moment after that, Froggat and Greening were back in the jollyboat. The joint would be put on His Majesty's account, against all regulations, and a shilling would go to any man or woman in the town who would cook the damned thing for us.

They returned with a basket of potatoes and turnips, and the welcome news that the clerk's wife would roast the joint on her hearth. For the remainder of the morning I allowed the hands to lounge like lords at their leisure and this they did with artful pleasure. A few dozed while others smoked or mended their clothes, their heads and spirits improving as the day wore on. Shortly after noon we saw a boy waving from shore, a signal that the food was ready. Bolger and Greening volunteered for the task and the rest of the crew sharpened their knives and whetted their appetites on a small ration of rum. The potatoes and turnips had been set to boil on the shallop's stove and everyone was in high good humour at the thought of the feast.

When next I looked, the jollyboat had put out for the return trip with the gunner sitting in the sternsheets, looking for all the world like the King's steward. He held the great steaming joint on a board across his knees while Greening bent his back to the oars. As inviting as the mutton looked, however, it was not the primary object of my attention, for I saw that we were soon to have a visitor. There was a third person in the boat, a woman who sat in the bow facing aft so that her face could not be seen. Her back was straight beneath a dark shawl and a plain grey bonnet covered her hair. I took her to be the clerk's wife, though why she needed to accompany the roast was a mystery to me. Perhaps she intended to haggle over her fee.

Derek Yetman

The jollyboat bumped alongside and the mutton was helped aboard by eager hands. The woman, her back to me, stood up and ignored Greening's clumsy attempt to assist her. She gathered her skirts and apron and stepped deftly over the centre thwart. As she turned, I felt a downward rush of blood that caused my head to swim and threatened to topple me over. The face that looked up at me was older, and yet it was the one I'd carried in my mind these many years. The golden curls had darkened and there were lines on the fair forehead but there was no mistaking that this was the face that I had loved and mourned by turns. The hazel eyes were unchanged and they held me like a boatswain's knot as she came handily up the side.

The blood returned to my head with a speed that matched its descent and I felt my face flush red. My voice abandoned me entirely and I stood as dumb as a plank while the men looked on with amused or curious glances. They did not watch for long, as Froggat had unsheathed a cutlass and was attacking the great lump of meat. The crew fell to like a flock of terns, leaving me alone with the apparition before me. Indeed, she might have been a spirit raised from my past, for she had yet to speak or do anything but hold my eyes with that unflinching stare. I was at a loss for something to say or do until I thought to invite her into the cabin. I found my voice and did just that, to grins and nudges among the crew. I held the door ajar and she bent her head to enter. Inside, I positioned a stool for her and sat myself on another with the low table between us. She sat and a long moment passed before she spoke. When she did, her voice was no louder than a whisper but I heard it well enough.

"May God damn your black heart, Jonah Squibb."

What had I expected her to say, when it came down to it? In my confusion, I had supposed she'd come aboard to say hello and to renew our acquaintance. I was, after all, an old childhood friend and she a respectable woman. I thought she might even say that it was nice to see me again. I was wrong, of course, and how wrong was made clear when she repeated her words in a louder voice. My tongue failed me still. Her face was a picture of sadness and hurt, though her eyes bore a hardness that hinted at an anger nurtured long and deep.

"Why did you never come back?" she demanded. "Why did I never hear from you again?"

I found my voice and replied, "Forgive me Amy, but—"

"Forgive you!" she cried. "I will never forgive you for what you did to me, sir."

"But ... but you chose to marry!" I protested. "You wrote to me. I still have the letter!"

"What did you expect of me, Jonah?" A tremor had crept into her voice. "After all them months and months of never hearing a word from you? Of running down to the landwash every time a boat or a ship come into the harbour, hoping it was carrying a letter for me? What did you expect? I thought you was dead. Or worse, that everything you'd told me was empty lies."

I drew a shallow, unsteady breath. "Amy, I did write to you. Upon my soul. I wrote often but some of my letters went astray, as will happen when war—"

"Yes, some might have gone astray," she shot back, "but what of the rest?" Her voice broke again as she fought to keep her composure.

"Others came back to me, Amy. I still have them."

In her eyes I saw a tiny flicker of doubt, the shock that a long-held conviction may have been mistaken. "You still have them?" she whispered.

I reached behind me and threw open the lid of my sea chest. From beneath a spare shirt and my volumes of Fielding and Smollett, I drew out a packet of letters tied in a blue ribbon. The ribbon was faded and the papers foxed and stained from dampness and sea air, but her name and address could still be read on the outer pages. I laid the packet on the table and she stared at it. When she reached out, ever so gently, to touch the frayed ends of the ribbon, I saw that her hands were rough and red from labour.

She said nothing, her lower lip between her teeth, until I untied the bow and offered her the topmost letter. It was one of the last I'd written at St. John's six years before and the page shook in her hand as she read it, her tearful eyes following my words. They declared my love and a pledge to marry her as soon as I could find my way to Trinity. The letter had never left my ship because of a scheming purser and an officer who had made my life a torment.

It was strange to see those words read at last by the one for whom they were intended. There was no joy or satisfaction to it, only sorrow and regret. I am certain that she felt it too, for she laid the letter aside and put her hands to her face. I gave her a kerchief and wiped my own eyes with the sleeve of my coat, the tears mingling with the crusted salt of the sea

The cocks crowed around the harbour as I stepped onto the beach at Mackerel Point. The Taverner plantation was a shambles compared to my memory of it. The once bountiful garden was choked with weeds and the roof of an old outbuilding had fallen in on itself. The house, which had been among the finest in the harbour, was missing a patch of wooden shingles and an upstairs window had been boarded over. For whatever reason, I felt a stab of guilt concerning Amy and her son. I walked up from the beach and knocked on a door that rattled in its frame.

If she were surprised to see me there was no hint of it, nor did she seem embarrassed by her circumstances. I had only to remove my hat and say good morning and she invited me in with a smile and a glance at her neighbours' windows. She led me to the kitchen and offered a chair, which I accepted, and a cup of tea, which I did not. We made some small talk about the weather and how the September gales would soon be upon us. There seemed to be little else to say after our long talk of the day before, and yet I had come here because of a sense of something left unsaid. Yesterday I had told her the story of my recent life and she had done me the favour of relating her own. She'd tried to put it all in a good light but behind her words I saw a life of poverty and struggle. It included a husband who had poured their meagre earnings down his throat and an uncle, as rich as he was, who offered nothing. Even after she was widowed, old Lester ignored her plight except to employ her at making fish for a penny a day. By contrast, the first thing I'd seen on entering the harbour was his fine new mansion at the foot of Ryder's Hill.

Her blonde-haired boy was there, watching me from the parlour doorway. He was about five years of age and his round cheeks and shy smile made me think of the Indian child. The dark cloud was about to revisit when her voice drew me back. She asked after my guardian, the Reverend Lindsey, and I told her that he had died these three years past. She did me the kindness of saying that he was remembered fondly and was greatly missed when he retired and returned to England.

Our conversation was restrained and polite, though my heart was pounding within me, and I dared to hope that all of the anger and pain of yesterday had been purged. On board the *Dove* we'd talked for nearly an hour and in the end we forgave each other for all the wrongs we'd imagined. In truth, our fates had been sealed through no fault of our own. Unhappy circumstance alone had intervened to take away the joy and promise of our young lives. But Lord, what I would not have given to go back in time and change all that had happened. I would have gone to Trinity as I'd intended, in spite of her letter, and we would have been married and happy these last six years.

But of course the past could not be changed. There was only the present, and I longed to say that I had thought of her every day for six years, but I did not. I opened my mouth to do so several times, and I believe she looked at me in expectation, but no words would come. My feelings had been bottled too long, and the cork would not come loose. In the end I took my leave without a word to her of my feelings. I was a fool, I know, if not a coward, and we parted with nothing more than a bow and a curtsey. She did say that she hoped we would meet again, and half an hour later I sailed from Trinity with a tortured heart.

For the whole of that day and half of the next, I spoke to

no one. After giving command to Froggat, I shut myself into the cabin to write my report and to think upon the two weeks that had passed since we departed St. John's. There had been little enough joy in that fortnight and I was deep in gloomy reflection before long. I might have remained there until we reached Toulinguet, were it not for the events of our second day at sea. We were off Cape Fogo with a rising glass when the French brigantine took wind of us again. Greening spied her a good way off, coming on from the northeast. I was summoned and my first act was to curse my complacency. Until then we had been sailing at our leisure with the waist full of stores and wood for the stove. As I surveyed the rapidly advancing vessel I knew that something would have to go by the board.

Greening and Grimes were ordered to jettison the firewood and supplies while the boatswain drove Rundle and Jenkins aloft to set the little topsail. Bolger began laying out powder and shot for the guns and Froggat and I consulted our chart. At a glance, we knew that we would have to run with the wind, straight into the Bay of Exploits. There we might stand a second, small chance of escaping among the islands that Captain Cook had marked so well.

Our speed increased with the added sail but Grimes was damnably slow in clearing the wood. Frost remedied his indolence with a piece of rope, and had he flayed him alive I would have held my tongue. The man was a festering boil upon our collective ass and my patience was nearing an end. If I sound cruel I cannot say otherwise with a clear conscience. Grimes had used up my store of civility and I was not about to spare him if it meant the difference between capture and escape.

The brig continued to gain and I knew that our load would have to be lightened further. Greening was working like a demon and timber was bobbing thick in our wake. I ordered the barrels of provisions over the side and Bolger and Frost hoisted the first cask to the bulwark and dropped it into the sea. Another followed and then another, until the deck was clear of all but our powder and shot, one small barrel of pork, some scraps of wood, and a sack of potatoes. I stopped the men there; we had established a separation of a thousand yards and were in no immediate danger from the *Valeur*'s guns. When that distance did not alter over the next hour, I told the men to organize a meal while they had the chance. What lay ahead was uncertain but it was a fair guess that there would be no time for eating.

Our wake was foaming white as they calmly fired the stove and Rundle took a hammer to the lid of our remaining barrel of pork. When it came loose we recoiled at the smell. Whether all of Lester's barrels were spoiled we would never know, but the thought crossed my mind that while fortune may have improved the man's circumstances, it had done nothing for his character. The lid was hastily replaced and the men made ready to tip it over the side when I stopped them. If there were even a few pieces unspoiled it could mean the difference between a hungry surrender and a long chance of escape. The hands ate their dinner as the chase wore on. There was grumbling, of course, for a seaman without good pork is a touchy beast. I reminded them all that they would eat much worse before their days in the Navy were ended. Once, on a bedeviled voyage to the Indies, my shipmates and I had eaten nothing for days but a cold, crawling mess of black-headed weevils. They were all that remained of the bread they had grown fat upon.

All that day we drove south and east, until sunset found us in the Reach, that familiar strait south of Chapel Island. Here I ordered our sails reefed with the coming darkness, assuming the brig would do the same. It was a gamble, but the greater risk lay in driving ashore, for the currents were unpredictable and the channel too narrow to manoeuvre in. At midnight the Frenchman fired a ranging shot to no effect, though it did rattle the men who'd gone to their hammocks for an hour's rest. Shortly before dawn Froggat called me aft and declared that they had begun to close the distance. It was still dark but I put my trust in his instincts and ordered Frost to let out the reefs without delay. The Frenchman may have had the same intuition, for he loosed another shot that threw up a plume of water a dozen yards from our stern.

Dawn brought the realization that the wind was failing. What was worse, it was localized and seemed to have less effect upon the progress of the other vessel. I called for the sweeps and the four seamen manned one apiece. The effort was largely in vain, however, and even with the warrant officers lending a hand we could not escape the *Valeur*'s range. Her next shot struck a glancing blow aft larboard, shivering a few of our timbers but causing no real damage.

Some would say that my next decision was rashly taken, though at that moment I saw it as a bold stroke that might win us some time. By then the fitful wind had disappeared entirely and the sea lay between us in a near calm. The Frenchman's sails were as slack as ours and they were preparing their sweeps as well. We had by then passed out of the Reach and were near Birchy Island with Shoal Tickle Point to larboard. Between these two lay Shoal Tickle itself, a tight little entry of one hundred yards width and no great depth, as its name implied. The tide being at the ebb, I urged the men to pull for all they were worth. I called to Bolger to make ready the aft starboard gun.

"Cartridge is pricked, sir," he said as I sighted along the barrel.

"I make it eight hundred yards, master gunner."

"Aye, sir," he said, looking at the brig, "and perhaps another twenty-five for good measure."

I grabbed the swivel's handle and made the adjustment. The barrel lay level with the sea. "Beggin' yer pardon, sir," the gunner said. "But a one-pounder with that charge will only make six hundred yards at fifteen degrees. That angle won't—"

He was silenced by the tremulous hum of a four-pound ball that passed no more than two or three feet above our heads. The wind of it sent his hat flying into the sea. "Stand by, tiller and sweeps," I called. The men rowed with determination while I watched the Frenchman and waited. We entered the tickle and the points of land on either side came amidships. I counted one, two, three strokes of the oars until we were clear.

"Belay larboard sweeps. Hard over tiller, Mister Froggat."

The shallop turned on a gold piece, straight for the shelter of Birchy Island. One, two, three strokes from the starboard side and I put the smoldering match to the touchhole. The swivel roared and the shot hit the flat water five hundred yards out. It ricocheted like a skipping stone in a series of diminishing arcs that might have carried it a thousand yards or more, had it not met with the bow of the *Valeur*. In a shower of sparks the ball severed the anchor chains and her best bower broke loose and plunged into the sea. The crew of the *Dove* gave an astonished cheer as we passed out of sight behind Birchy Island.

"I'll be a spiny dogfish!" the gunner declared. "I seen it done before but never with a blessed swivel. Upon my word, young sir! Well done!"

The men laughed and whooped but I told them to pull for their liberty, if not their lives. The shot had been no more than bravado, fired in hopes of angering the Frenchman into rash pursuit. It was a gamble with poor odds but with the tide at its ebb I was betting that the brig would draw more water than was in the tickle. A gentle waft of air lifted our topsail and Froggat worked the tiller to take full advantage of it. My immediate concern was to remove the *Dove* from harm's way, should the *Valeur* either pass through the channel unimpeded or run aground with its four-pound guns blazing away at us. The Spruce Islands lay about a league distant and their shelter was our only sanctuary.

With the help of the rising breeze we were halfway there when the Frenchman entered Shoal Tickle. Just as I'd hoped, her captain had thrown caution to the wind and was taking the channel with all the speed he could muster. I watched from the stern of our little shallop and hardly dared to breathe. Froggat stood beside me with his knuckles white on the tiller. On came the brig, even as I wished aloud that she would seize the bottom and rattle her masts. On and on she came without so much as a scrape, until she had cleared the Tickle and was coming up fast in our wake.

The French captain had either sailed Shoal Tickle before, or else he was the luckiest man afloat. The brig passed through it without so much as a scratch to her keel, and then celebrated by firing her guns at us. I gave new thought to our situation as a plunging shot threw a spray of water over the deck. The Spruce Islands were still half a league away with the wind rising on the starboard quarter. The islands were the largest part of a maze of rocks and shoals, and in these I placed our final hope.

The Frenchman kept up his ragged fire but the standard of gunnery was a scandal. Four-pound balls dropped into the sea on all sides of us, none but the first coming close enough to remark upon. Over the next half-hour the wind continued to rise and the sea to build, until the *Dove* was pitching sharply in the deepening troughs. My plan, such as it was, involved leading the brig among the islands and as close to the rocks as I dared, again on the chance that she might strike bottom and be damned. This would be risky enough in light airs, but now the sea was becoming capricious.

The waves in fact seemed to be heralding something of a squall. "Like dogs before their master," I heard Froggat say. As we passed the first of the Spruce Islands, the wind brought drizzle and fog swiftly into the bay, quickly obscuring the rocky knoll. Treacherous shoals now lay all around us and I gave Froggat a heading that would take us deeper within the labyrinth.

The *Valeur* kept up her occasional fire until she suddenly luffed up into the wind and gave us a single broadside. Three of the balls thrummed harmlessly overhead, but the fourth spelled the end of able seaman Rundle. I had ordered the *Dove* about on the larboard tack a moment before and it was a lucky shot that found him. He was standing in the shrouds, reaching for the topsail sheet, when the unseen ball took away his arm. At first there was scarcely any blood, owing to the shock of it, but it came fast enough when he fell to the deck. Frost tried to staunch the flow with the shirt from his own back but the little Cornishman died some few minutes later. I have to say that I was sorry to see him pass. In life he scarcely had the sense to know his duty, and yet I think he might have done well enough, had he been removed from the influence of Grimes. Jenkins sobbed as he helped put the body over the side, but Grimes did not give his old shipmate as much as a departing glance.

With the wind and rain upon us, we ran before the squall with jib and reefed mainsail alone, the topsail having threatened to part or take away the mast. Frost had rigged a reefing jackstay for extra support but I was not convinced that it would take the strain. All the while I kept a close eye on the brig and was happy to see that her seamanship was showing again. Canvas went up and down according to a momentary gust and the vessel yawed like a drunken sailor.

As dusk approached the wind dropped a few knots and turned a point to the west. Darkness descended quickly and the sky merged with the sea while I resisted the urge to crowd more canvas. We were south of Upper Black Island and I knew that Lobster Rock was somewhere near, dangerous and invisible in the night. The wind turned another point and the rain gradually lessened. Stars appeared and the moon broke through the clouds to illuminate the bay in a wash of silvery light. I had taken up my compass to try and fix our position when I heard Jenkins shouting from the bows. I looked up, and as I did the light of the moon revealed a sight that nearly caused my heart to stop. Dead ahead, and not more than a biscuit toss away, was the Lobster, a tiny speck on my chart that now loomed as large as a continent.

"Helm a-lee!" I cried. Froggat did so in an instant and the sudden change in direction nearly threw Greening from the masthead, where he'd been watching for the brig.

"Deck ahoy!" he called when he'd recovered his hold. We were then shaving past the foaming rocks with not a dozen yards to spare. If I heard his cry it did not register, occupied as I was in willing us to safety. "Deck ahoy!" he roared again. "Sail on the starboard beam!"

This time his words forced me to tear my eyes from the breakers. There, out of the darkness and bearing down with

Derek Yetman

stunning speed, was the Frenchman. He'd thrown caution to the wind and was upon us with the weather gauge in his favour. I could not manoeuvre without allowing him to change course the more easily and intercept us on his own terms. We were in as tight a spot as any I could imagine, and yet I was unwilling to surrender without a fight.

"Bear off the wind, Mister Froggat," I said, hoping my voice sounded calm. By wearing ship I hoped to round the Lobster , away from the brig to prevent its broadside from coming into play. "Set topsail, boatwsain. Ready the guns, Mister Bolger. All hands stand by."

We were now running before the wind but a glance astern told me that it was not enough. The Frenchman had three times our sail and nothing could prevent him from overtaking us. It was now a question of which side he would engage us on. The moon's light showed clearly the faces of my crew as they stood at their quarters. The warrant officers looked grim but determined and young Greening was fidgeting with nervous excitement. Jenkins waited, open-mouthed and staring, while Grimes wiped his palms repeatedly on his breeches. Cutlasses and pistols had been laid near at hand and I quickly tucked a primed piece into my belt.

"Are you ready, Mister Froggat?"

He nodded and heartened me with his reply: "Dying is of no importance, Jonah, for it lasts so short a time."

I smiled at his paraphrase of Johnson and turned to the business of drawing all that we could from our little sloop, for sloop was how I now thought of her. In the last few days no humble shallop could have served us so well, and I thought it only fitting that she be accorded some dignity before being sent to the bottom.

The Frenchman now made his intentions known, altering course to come abeam on our larboard side. At my word the crew rallied to our two small guns. Every man expected the worst as the brig drew abreast, but then, just at the critical moment, we witnessed a sight that caused us to stare in disbelief. In altering course her crew missed stays and lost so much of her headway that she dropped astern again. It was an unexpected deliverance, but one that merely delayed the inevitable.

While this was absorbing our attention there was treachery afoot on board the *Dove*. All hands were watching the antics of the Frenchman while Grimes was climbing unseen onto the forecastle with a cutlass in his hand. There he began hacking at our jib sheets and halyards with clear intent to disable us. I turned at the first sound and my reaction was immediate: I drew the pistol from my belt and levelled it at his back.

As the senior officer, the blame was mine alone. I was wrong to trust Grimes in the working of the ship, even when there were so many mistrustful eyes to watch him. His intention could only have been to deliver us into the hands of the French, and in doing so to escape the justice that awaited him. It was even likely that he'd lost his reason, for John Wilkes' influence had twisted his mind in dangerous directions. Whatever his motive, it was now my firm intent to put a ball between his shoulder blades. My finger tightened on the trigger, even as Greening leapt upon the forecastle and obstructed my line of fire. I saw him raise his boot to the worn seat of Grimes' pants, and with arms flailing the traitor flew head first over the bow. A scream cut short was the last we knew of him.

Or so I thought. In fact, he did not plunge into the sea at all. It was only as Frost and Greening began knotting and repairing the sheets and halyards that they discovered him hanging over the side, his foot entangled in the ropes that he'd hacked from the rigging. His fall had been arrested just short of the waves and his body had slammed with great force into the bow timbers. He hung there unconscious, his head and arms dragging in foam from our bow wave. Greening picked up the cutlass and stood over the rope. A single chop and Grimes would cease to exist. I saw him hesitate, and may God forgive me but I said nothing. To the man's great credit, and to my shame, he threw the blade aside and took hold of the rope, his broad back straining as he drew the unconscious Judas onto the deck.

Derek Yetman

Our jib was now trailing over the bow and checking our way, and Frost stood out on the plunging bowsprit to gather it in. It was a valiant act, though ultimately pointless, because it was the last thing he ever did upon this earth. With our speed diminished the *Valeur* had come up quickly on our starboard side. Without warning, her broadside thundered from sixty yards away. One shot passed between Froggat and myself, close enough to make my eyes water with the rush of air. Another holed us at the waterline and a third smashed through the gunwale, dismounting number three swivel and impaling Jenkins' thigh with a two-foot splinter of wood. The fourth ball struck our bow, taking away the sprit and part of the stem. The boatswain went with it, and there was no question of his having survived. A great spray of blood on the flapping staysail was all that remained. We had no time to mourn his passing, or even to think of his loss, for the French were already reloading their guns.

From the stern deck I looked down on a moonlit scene of frenzy and destruction. Jenkins writhed and screamed in the debris while Greening and Bolger struggled to clear the other gun. To fight on would be suicide, I knew, but I intended to make a final statement before pulling down our ensign. At my order the gunner pointed number one swivel and fired into the enemy. His shot bounced off her tumblehome and deflected upwards, severing the chain on her foremast yard.

It was very strange that in the midst of all of this I should think of Amy Taverner. My heart was racing, my eyes burning from the smoke and my every sense attuned to the peril of our situation. And yet the notion that I would never see her again had entered my head, along with a feeling of calm acceptance. It passed over me like a wave and was gone in an instant, but the knowledge that I had experienced it lingered much longer. I looked across to the brig, where the French were clumsily pointing their weapons. Our own gun was ready for a second salvo and Bolger was waiting to time it with our roll. With the loss of the jib we were moving in every direction and he waited for what seemed an eternity until the right angle came

The Beothuk Expedition

to bear. The ball struck what remained of the stays on their foremast yard and it toppled to the deck in a tangle of ropes, canvas and scrambling men. I threw the rudder over and we sheered away, filling our sails and putting our stern to the brig before her guns could reply.

I had no way of knowing it then, but the gunner's shot would hamper the *Valeur* enough for us to put some miles between us. By the same token, however, I had no way of knowing that one of her guns would first wreak havoc upon us. In a surprising show of accuracy or good luck, the hissing ball took us square astern. It entered the aft cabin below my feet with a deadly shower of splinters and shards and passed through the full length of the sloop. Every man in the waist was struck by the wreckage, though by some miracle they were all left alive. The most seriously hurt was Bolger, who was thumped on the head by a stout piece of oak and was missing a good piece of his scalp. The ball passed into the forecastle cabin and lodged in our bow timbers, shaking loose a few planks but leaving us in no danger of sinking.

It was the final shot of the skirmish, for it can hardly be called a battle. With the disabled *Valeur* dead in the water we limped northward, never keeping our heading for more than a minute because of the missing bowsprit. We zigzagged out of the Bay of Exploits, fluttering like an injured waterfowl and fearing that the predator would return for the kill. The men were in a sorry state, bruised and battered, and I called for a double ration of rum to bring them around. It was the only thing that remained of our provisions, the barrel of dodgy pork having been blown to kingdom come.

I made my way forward to the gunner and found him conscious and lucid. As I inspected his wound he spoke with sadness of his old friend Frost, and all they had been through together. "Why, sir," he said as I inspected his torn scalp, "him and me was boys together in the *Leopard* when Cap'n Palliser were a midshipman. Frost used to say he were bred to the sea on account o' his mother being a mermaid. A fine man before the mast, was Hard Frost. He could hand, reef and steer before he were old enough to shave, and now me old shipmate's gone and entered the port o' heaven."

"We shall all miss him, master gunner," I assured him as I dabbed at the wound.

"He had a wife somewheres. Portsmouth, I think. He only seen her every three years or so, but I'd best try to find her all the same. I wonders sometimes if he didn't know that his end were nigh. 'Twere something he said to me when we was about to fight that brig. It were one o' them foolish rhymes 'o his: *Sailing, sailing over the bounding main, Many a stormy wind shall blow 'Ere Jack comes home again*. Funny, ain't it, sir? Like he knew he'd be clewing up his topsails afore long. And who can say? Maybe that's how it is for us all when our time is up."

I left Bolger with his sorrow and another tot of rum before inspecting the damage fore and aft. A jagged hole gaped in the stern bulwark, throwing light upon a jumble of broken wood and torn hammocks. Everything in there had been smashed except my old sea chest, which had acquired a few new scars. The ball had exited the cabin and only nicked the mast in passing forward, which was another stroke of good luck. I put my head into the space beneath the forecastle and saw that it was equally ravaged. The door had been blown inward, shredding the hammocks that still hung from the beams and tearing apart the crew's bags and chests. The four-pound shot was clearly visible, embedded between the stem and the connecting timbers. All this I saw at a glance, my attention being drawn to the sight of Jenkins on hands and knees in the rubble, blood seeping from the wound in his thigh. In the cabin's dim light he was clawing through the mess, completely oblivious to my presence. Only then did I notice the pungently bitter aroma that penetrated the dust and smoke. The smell was vaguely familiar.

Mine are not the keenest of wits, I will admit. For weeks the clues had been mounting around me and I'd been as blind as a jellyfish. Only at that moment did the truth finally dawn upon me, the smell transporting me back to the surgeon's house in Bonavista. A woman was handing me a bowl of powdered medication and saying that the surgeon had been giving it to Froggat.

At my feet, Jenkins licked the boards of a shattered sea chest and whimpered like a child.

After two days of makeshift repairs and graceless sailing, we rounded the southern tip of Fogo Island. The sun was level with our stern rail and in the fading light we saw the squadron lying at our rendezvous in Man o' War Cove. They were all there—the *Guernsey*, *Liverpool*, *Lark*, and *Tweed*—every spar properly squared and the sailors lining the decks to watch our strange little craft. I thought of a line from Fielding's *Journal*, in which he rightly observed that a fleet of ships is the noblest thing that the art of man has ever produced. The sight of so much strength and order cheered us, in spite of the poor spectacle we made. We must have looked like castaways, with our clothes torn and stiff with dried blood and salt, and ourselves haggard from want of food and sleep. The *Dove* herself was a woeful sight, her shot holes patched with scraps of wood and a ragged wound where her bowsprit should have been. All the same, I was proud of that little sloop and doubly so of her valiant crew.

Froggat put us alongside the *Guernsey* and I climbed the sidesteps with some effort to where Mr. Cartwright and Mr. Tench were waiting. The latter said nothing, neither welcoming nor acknowledging me, his gaze as ill-disposed as ever. Even Lieutenant Cartwright received me rather formally, I thought, after all that we had been through together. Still, he could not hide the anxiety in his voice as he asked me what news I had of the Indian child. It was passing strange that he did not inquire after the health of the men or notice that two of their number were missing. I told him what I knew and his shoulders fell as he listened. I could see that his failure upon the river lay heavily upon him.

My words were listened to intently by Lieutenant Tench as well, and I imagined a brief hint of a smile on his stony countenance. I made my way to Captain Palliser's cabin where he received me with great civility and listened carefully to my report. On hearing that I'd lost two men to the *Valeur* he scowled but said little, except to regret the loss of his boatswain. He remarked that Frost's character may have been improvable but in the final sum he had been a fine sailor and an asset to the *Guernsey*. As for the *Valeur*, he said that he would dispatch the *Lark* straight away to search for her. Our noble frigate would have no joy, however, for a week later the Frenchman was spotted on the Grand Banks, sailing hard for France.

On the subject of the child, the captain made no comment, other than to shake his head gravely. I could not help but wonder if he acknowledged the error of his reward or if he still held to its merit. I did suggest that the authorities at Poole be alerted, even though the message would arrive weeks after the ship in question. We both knew how unlikely the child's recovery was, but he said that he would do everything in his power. The news that the furriers had evaded me drew no response, as if he'd expected as much. I felt badly enough about it, although I knew there was nothing I could have done to change the outcome.

On the greater issue of the Red Indians, I told him with all respect that if something were not done their race would soon be harried to extinction. He heard me out and even acknowledged the truth of my prediction. In a weary voice he told me he'd been petitioning the Admiralty and Lords on this very matter since he became governor. What I had so clearly stated was obvious to any who had served on the Newfoundland station, he said, but the matter was as nothing to those in London. In governing an empire that would soon span the globe there were many things that did not receive the attention they deserved. There were more pressing issues in England itself, not least the public disorder being incited by John Wilkes. I apologized for my presumption but he waved it away, saying this was another argument against year-round settlement of the island. When the squadron departed in the fall there was nothing to deter those who remained, including those who would see the natives destroyed.

The Beothuk Expedition

Captain Palliser then turned to the subject of Grimes, who was at that moment being taken aboard the *Guernsey* in irons. Lieutenant Cartwright had provided an account of his suspected involvement in the Indian murder and abduction and I now recounted his actions during our encounter with the brig. The governor listened carefully, and then rang a small silver bell that summoned his clerk to the cabin. The order was given that Grimes would appear before a court martial the following morning, charged with treason and attempting to aid and abet the enemy. By my own reckoning, three and possibly four of the Articles of War had been violated, which made the verdict a certainty.

The clerk withdrew and Mr. Palliser gave his attention to a document on his desk. I assumed the interview to have ended and made my bow to leave. It was then that I remembered to ask whether Froggat and Jenkins ought be returned to the *Liverpool*. I also enquired as to what should be done with the damaged sloop. Mr. Palliser rubbed his leg and considered the question.

"They may return to their ship if they desire," he said. "Or else they may remain with you."

I did not reply because I was at a loss to understand his meaning. Nor did I move to go, even as he returned to his document. An awkward moment passed while he picked up a quill and dipped it in ink to affix his signature. "Mister Squibb," he said, "I am resolved to bring the rule of law to this coast, with or without the support of London. However, I cannot spare even one of my frigates for the task, not with so vast an area to patrol." He handed me the paper and I took it, wondering what all of this had to do with me.

"In view of the situation," the governor continued, "I am giving you an acting appointment as chief naval officer and surrogate judge for the coast, from Trinity to Toulinguet, and beyond, if the situation demands. You will remain with your vessel, with a fresh crew and larger guns, of course. You may not keep my gunner, however. He must be returned to the *Guernsey* immediately." He paused and looked me in the eye. "Well, sir? What have you to say?"

I was astounded, naturally enough Somehow I managed to say that I was honoured by his trust, as indeed I was. It was a singular thing for a junior lieutenant to be given such a responsibility and I stammered something about more deserving officers than myself. Fortunately the governor's attention had returned to his desk and he seemed not to hear. I took my leave, bowing as I backed from the cabin and nearly upsetting a stand of charts by the door.

Froggat and Greening were waiting for me on deck and when I told them the news they congratulated me with honest good will. In the next breath they both declared their intention of remaining with the sloop. I was touched by their loyalty and thanked them sincerely, especially as I would be relying upon their skills and support. Still incredulous but reassured by the faith placed in me, I made my weary way to my old cabin deep within the *Guernsey*. It was just as I'd left it weeks before, the sailcloth walls still taut and everything in good order. Calling the steward, I ordered a bath and removed my clothes, the man swearing that he would sooner burn them than see them washed. After this my thoughts turned to other needs, a meal and sleep being foremost. I had stood watch for the better part of three days without a morsel and was in danger of dropping where I stood. I made my way to the wardroom and there I ate the better part of a stewed goat, washed down with a bottle of claret. Afterwards I dragged myself to my berth and slept for twelve straight hours, waking the next morning to a great clamour and banging alongside.

My first thought on opening my eyes was not of the noise, nor of anything immediate to my senses. It was of Amy Taverner. I now regretted my hesitation in Trinity, and was plagued by the thought that I should have spoken of my feelings. What if she did harbour some sentiment for me? Perhaps I had missed something in her manner, some subtle hint or intonation. The idea filled me with alarm and confused my memory of what had actually passed between us. The harder I tried to remember, the less I was able to recall. Finally, and rashly, I formed the notion that I ought to visit her again, that I might know her mind, and her heart, more clearly. I lay thinking on it for some time, until confusion got the better of me and I dressed and went up to the quarterdeck.

The source of the noise that had awoken me was soon obvious, for looking over the side I saw a crew of boatswain's and carpenter's mates swarming about the *Dove*. They had repaired and improved the little sloop almost beyond recognition. There was a new bowsprit and rigging, freshly planed wood and never a sign of a shot hole. The carpenter himself appeared and invited me on board to inspect the repairs. I descended the rope ladder and was surprised to find the little sloop fully provisioned and crewed by half a dozen volunteers. In fact, apart from the *Guernsey*'s people gathering up their tools, she was ready to sail at a word from me.

I had no time to bask in the glory of my new command, however, for I had several things that demanded my attention. With Greening's help I winkled Jenkins out from the *Guernsey*'s lower deck where he lay shivering and moaning in a darkened corner. I had Greening take him on board the *Dove* while I proceeded to the sick berth. There I found the ship's aged surgeon in his little dispensary, counting leeches in a jar. When I presented him with a sample of the powder that had been in Grimes' shattered sea chest, he sniffed it once and put it to his tongue. Taking up a vial from a row on his desk, he uncorked it and passed it to me. The identically bitter pungence wafted past my nose.

"Powder of opium" he croaked. "*Opii pulvis*. A most effective sedative and surgical anesthetic. But it must be used sparingly, of course. It is highly addictive."

His words were the glue that bound the pieces together. In Bonavista, with the collusion of that wretched surgeon, Grimes had kept Froggat in a state of insensibility while they made merry with his money. And Rundle and Jenkins had been under his influence, not by the threat of violence as I had supposed, but by their dependence upon him for the opiate. Froggat had told me of the *Liverpool*'s cruise to the Far East and that must have been where the substance was acquired and where their addiction began.

I left the surgeon to his leeches and made my way to the captain's cabin, where the court martial of Nehemiah Grimes was about to begin. His own captain from the *Liverpool*, the governor and another officer made up the tribunal, while the accused stood before them, hobbled and flanked by a pair of red-coated marines. I took my place at the back of the room alongside Lieutenants Cartwright and Tench as the charges were read. My statement was then entered into the record and Froggat and Bolger were called upon to confirm the account of events on board the *Dove*. Grimes listened with a contemptuous scowl, the chains clanking when he moved his feet. After hearing the evidence, the court asked if he had anything to say in his own defence.

"Wilkes and freedom!" was his reply, shouted to the court. The marines stepped closer and seized his arms. The three officers conferred for a moment, and Mr. Palliser stood up.

"Nehemiah Grimes, petty officer of HMS *Liverpool*." There was complete silence, even from Grimes. "The court finds you guilty of violating Articles eleven, twelve and fourteen of the code that governs His Majesty's naval service. To whit, you have failed to obey the orders of a superior officer for joining battle with a ship, and have presumed to submit a vessel of His Majesty's service to peril. Further to this, you are found guilty of harbouring and acting upon a traitorous and mutinous design."

The governor grimaced and shifted his weight to his good leg. "To answer for these crimes," he concluded, "you will be hanged by the neck until dead. The sentence will be carried out at sunrise tomorrow."

Grimes seemed too shocked to move for a moment. But then he was struggling against the grip of his guards and crying, "No justice, no king!" He called upon the marines to overthrow their common oppressor, a plea that earned him a sharp elbow to the ribs. I felt a brief stab of pity that a sailor should have to die for falling under the spell of a politician's

The Beothuk Expedition

empty rhetoric. But then I thought of my old friend Frost and the Indian woman, and the boy whose fate we would probably never know. The real pity, I thought, was that Grimes could only be hanged once.

With the prisoner subdued, the governor asked if he had anything to say to the court. Grimes lifted his head and looked around the cabin. I have no doubt that the man was deranged, possibly from the knowledge that he was soon to die, but his bitter laughter filled the room and unsettled me. His eyes scanned the faces that surrounded him and came to rest on the man standing next to me.

"You must be Tench," he said. All eyes turned to see a look of alarm spreading across the second lieutenant's face. "It's you, ain't it?" Grimes persisted.

"Mister Palliser!" Tench croaked as he found his voice. "I must protest, sir! The prisoner has no right to—"

"Cooper and Rowsell," Grimes said in a louder voice, "they was Pinson's men. And you're one, too."

The shocked silence of the room lasted until Tench, his face glowing scarlet, cried, "Sir! This is an outrage!"

Grimes turned a challenging glare to Mr. Cartwright, who was standing at my other side. "How else did the furriers know where to find you, eh? They was told you'd be at Fogo and that's where they was sent! Pinson knew you'd need to hire guides, and sure enough, there was Tom Rowsell. Only Sam Cooper got there late and had to follow you to Indian Point, now didn't he?"

I heard his words clear enough, but my mind was spinning as I tried to grasp their meaning. Captain Palliser's expression was frightening and Mr. Cartwright had lost his colour.

"I must insist, sir!" Tench shouted. "This man is condemned to death and will say anything to—"

The governor's even louder voice overrode his words. "What are you alleging, Grimes?"

"Pinson knew all about this plan to make peace with the Indians and to give 'em protection. Someone was passin' that on to 'im." The seaman smirked at Tench, whose face had taken on a purple hue. "And Pinson wasn't too happy with that news, now was he? It was goin' to interfere with him trappin' where he liked, and gettin' rid of them nuisance Indians. So he sent Cooper and Rowsell to scupper it all. If they killed an Indian or two then there'd never be a treaty, 'cause they'd never trust Cartwright, nor anyone else, again."

"What proof do you have of this?" Mr. Palliser demanded.

Grimes shook his head and gave a scornful laugh. "My proof is far away from here. In them woods. And only Pinson knows where for certain, or maybe his man here." He nodded towards Tench.

The second lieutenant made a strangled noise. His eyes were bulging with outrage or panic and I saw them dart to the cutlass rack on the wall. He began to sputter but the captain cut him short: "Enough, sir!" The anger in his voice was barely restrained. "I will deal with this anon, but for the moment it changes nothing in regard to this court martial. The charges against the prisoner have been proved, and he remains guilty. Take him below. He will be hanged on the morrow."

The court was dismissed, and each of us was left to ponder what we had heard. I did not sleep that night, nor, I am certain, did Mr. Cartwright. The possibility that we had been manipulated from the very beginning of our expedition was too much to accept, or even to comprehend. It was no secret that many were opposed to peace with the Red Indians, but never had I imagined the extent of that feeling or the effort to prevent it. The possibility that powerful merchants and navy officers were colluding for that purpose came as a great shock to me. Was it an isolated incident or was it pervasive? If it were true, how long had it been going on? Years, or decades? Or even, God help us, from the very beginning of our presence on the island? It was a long and troublesome night, not least because it seemed that we would never know the truth.

The next morning, shortly after Nehemiah Grimes had been raised to the yardarm by his neck, Lieutenant Tench climbed over the *Guernsey*'s side and into a waiting cutter, preceded by his sea chest and dunnage. He was rowed to the *Tweed*, where he would serve out the remainder of the voyage as a supernumerary officer with no responsibilities. This, I gathered, had been the result of a thunderous session in the captain's cabin, and I answered Mr. Palliser's summons with some trepidation a short time later.

As it was, I had no reason for anxiety. Mr. Cartwright was with the captain, and I saw that his dejection was now complete. The failure of his mission, the treachery of our own party, and now the possible deceit of a fellow officer had broken his will entirely. The governor was more angry than morose, and he wanted to know when I would be ready to part company in the *Dove*. I told him that I would be ready to sail at noon, and to this he nodded and stared at the papers on his desk.

I stood there for some moments before he took notice of me again, and looking up, he said, "Do not think badly of me, Mister Squibb." I was astonished to hear such a thing and stammered that I had never entertained the thought, nor saw any reason to do so. The governor shook his head and sighed.

"All the same, there are those who will say that I should have known better. There is the matter of the reward, for one. And for another, I had heard rumours of Tench's connections and interests some time ago. I cannot say that these were disreputable, but they were by no means transparent. I had little doubt that he was lining his own pockets, though by what means, I could only speculate. Even today, I have no proof of anything that Grimes has alleged."

The governor sat in quiet reflection for a moment before passing a hand over his face and clearing his throat. "I can say no more, gentlemen. Our attempt has come to nothing, and it may have made a grave situation worse. So there you have it."

The *Guernsey*'s midshipmen were shooting the noonday sun when Froggat came down the ladder and onto the stern of the *Dove*. Greening was standing beside me, polishing the glass of a new binnacle while I surveyed the rigging aloft.

Derek Yetman

"Captain Squibb?" I heard Froggat say, not for the first time that day. I had not been elevated in rank, but having command of the sloop, I was technically her captain and therefore, as a courtesy, could be addressed as such. Greening turned his back to hide a grin and I wondered how long they would keep this up.

"I make it noon, captain," Froggat said.

"Do you indeed?" I replied dryly.

"Everything squared and awaiting your orders, sir."

"We shall cast off in ten minutes, Mister Froggat."

"Aye, aye, captain."

I gave him a withering look before turning away to the towering bulk of the *Guernsey*. There was a small commotion at the rail and I looked up to see Reverend Stow perilously descending the rope ladder, assisted by the gunner. I had been expecting them to come aboard at my invitation, to drink a parting glass to our friendship. They descended onto the deck without injury, joking that they feared being abducted again. I assured them that it was more than my skin was worth even to contemplate such a thing.

Reverend Stow offered me the warmest congratulations and good wishes and Bolger expressed his disappointment at not being allowed to join us. I did not say it aloud but I regretted the captain's order equally as much. We drank a toast to one another and then a second glass to the memory of our friend, Hard Frost. After this we exchanged our goodbyes and the chaplain was about to ascend the ladder when he suddenly turned and declared, "May God bless the *Dove* and all who sail in her!"

The crew cheered and rushed to help him as he awkwardly mounted the ropes. The gunner went behind him to offer advice and I watched until they were safely aboard. Froggat, ever ready and efficient, ordered our lines cast off.

"What course, sir?" he asked as the crew rattled up the canvas.

I squinted into the pale sun that hovered above the mast while the little sloop began to gather way. "Shape a southeasterly course, Mister Froggat."

His gaze lingered a moment, as though he expected me to say something more.

Author's Note

On the 24th day of August, 1768, Lieutenant John Cartwright and thirteen others began the first European exploration of the Exploits River. Cartwright had been instructed by Governor Hugh Palliser to establish friendly relations with the Beothuk, or Red Indians, who were locked in a cycle of theft and retribution with trappers and fishermen. Palliser was the first naval governor to express concern over the fate of the island's indigenous people, and in John Cartwright he found an officer of similar views.

Under the guidance of planter John Cousens from Indian Point (now Cull's Point), Cartwright sailed a boat belonging to HMS *Liverpool* to Peter's Arm in the Bay of Exploits. Proceeding from there to Start Rattle, he began his historic journey on foot. Six days of arduous travel later, only five of the original party arrived at the source of the river. Cartwright named the body of water Lieutenant's Lake (now Red Indian Lake) but he found no evidence that the Beothuk had been there since the previous winter. This led him to conclude that the tribe was migratory and spent its summers on the coast.

It is surprising that Cartwright was unaware of this migratory pattern. He had stopped at Fogo en route to the Bay of Exploits and had talked with Tom June, referred to as "Cousens' Indian" in his diary. Some ten years earlier, in the month of June, the boy had been abducted by Irish hunters during an attack on his family's encampment. June later came into the employ of Cousens and worked as a fisherman out of Fogo. He provided Cartwright with a description of the lake but apparently neglected to tell him that his people would not be there in late August. Why he withheld that vital piece of information remains a mystery.

Tom June was the first Beothuk to live among Europeans. He is said to have been an expert in all branches of the fishery, even serving as master of a fishing vessel. Some time after his meeting with John Cartwright, he was drowned while negotiating the difficult entrance to Fogo Harbour.

At roughly the same time that Cartwright was on the river, a Beothuk woman was fatally shot by furriers and her male child abducted. Little more is known of the event, though Cartwright described the atrocity in passionate terms, illustrating the depth of his feeling for the natives' plight:

> *How the infant's cries, as they bore it off, must have pierced her faint heart! How the terrors of its approaching fate must have wrung a mother's breast ... what feeling, what mode of disgust has nature implanted in the human heart, to express its abhorrence of the wretch who can be so hardened to vice as to conceive that he is entitled to a reward for the commission of such bloody deeds!*
>
> *One of the very villains concerned in this capture of the child, supposing it a circumstance that would be acceptable to the Governor, actually came to the writer of these remarks at Toulinguet [now Twillingate], to ask a gratuity for the share he had borne in the transaction. Had he been describing the death of a beast of chase, and the taking of its young, he could not have shown greater insensibility than he did at the relation above mentioned.*
>
> *The woman was shot in August 1768, and to complete the mockery of human misery, her child was the winter following exposed as a curiosity to the rabble of Poole at two pence apiece.*

Whether the child's abductors were ever caught or punished is unclear, and unlikely. John August, as the four-year old Beothuk became known, was brought back to Newfoundland and, like Tom June, put to work in the fishery. He was first employed by Mr. Child at Catalina and later by the firm of Jeffrey and Street at Trinity. He died in 1788, was thought to have been twenty-four, and was interred in the Trinity churchyard. He was said to have returned to the river and to his people in the fall of each year.

Predictably, such murders and abductions intensified the cycle of violence between Beothuk and European. The capture of Tom June ten years earlier was followed by the killing of a shipmaster named Scott and five of his crew in the Bay of Exploits, and by the murder of Captain Hall in Hall's Bay. The abduction of John August, the death of his mother and other atrocities may have been avenged in 1789, when a furrier named Thomas Rowsell was killed in New Bay. A few years later, another furrier named Cooper was killed in Notre Dame Bay. Both had been known for their hatred of the native people. According to a contemporary account, friends of the two men avenged their deaths with "a war of extermination." The war lasted another forty years, until Shanawdithit, the last known member of her tribe, died of tuberculosis in 1829.

John Cartwright's thirteen companions on the river included Reverend Neville Stow, chaplain of the *Guernsey*, and George Cartwright, who later became a failed merchant on the coast of Labrador. On leave from the army, George had accompanied his brother for adventure, though he would later become an advocate for peaceful (and commercial) relations with the Red Indians.

Hugh Palliser was in the final year of his governorship in 1768, and his successor at last issued the proclamation of native protection that he had drafted. It had little effect, though Palliser's attempts to improve the welfare of both the Beothuk and the indentured fishermen of the island were remarkable for the period. History also records his opposition to permanent settlement in Newfoundland and his energetic dealings with the French over the terms of the Treaty of Paris.

John Cartwright returned to the island in 1769 and several years later resigned the Royal Navy rather than fight the Americans in their War of Independence. He was distinguished throughout his life for his humanitarian principles and keen sense of justice, and is remembered for having protected the poor Irish of Newfoundland from their often abusive employers (Andrew Pinson being recorded as one of the worst). Cartwright also wrote widely against slavery and in favour of American independence. Elected to the English Parliament in 1818, he was arrested and tried for sedition in 1820. He was convicted of attempting to persuade others to criticize the government and constitution and was fined one hundred pounds. He died in 1824 and a statue was erected to his memory in Cartwright Gardens, London, north of Russell Square.

Much of the detail for this novel has been drawn from the journal of John Cartwright and from the records of George Cartwright, Hugh Palliser, Joseph Banks and others. In many cases, the words of the characters have been taken directly from those documents.

Derek Yetman
St. John's, Newfoundland
October 2011

𝒟𝑒𝑟𝑒𝑘 𝒴𝑒𝑡𝑚𝑎𝑛 has been a writer, editor and journalist for more than thirty years. His interest in Newfoundland military and naval history began when he was a naval reservist and an officer of the Royal Newfoundland Regiment. His attachment to the nautical world continues as secretary of the Crow's Nest Officers' Club and as skipper of the sailboat *Second Wind*. He lives in St. John's. *The Beothuk Expedition* is his fourth novel.